Copyright © Matt Shaw 20

Cover art copyright © Matt Shaw Publications
Published: February, 2016
Publisher: Matt Shaw Publications

The right of Matt Shaw to be identified as author of this Work has been asserted by him in accordance with the Copyright, Designs and Patents Act 1988.

All rights reserved.
This eBook is copyright material and must not be copied, reproduced, transferred, distributed, leased, licensed or publicly performed or used in any way except as specifically permitted in writing by the publishers, as allowed under the terms and conditions under which it was purchased or as strictly permitted by applicable copyright law. Any unauthorised distribution or use of this text may be a direct infringement of the author's and publisher's rights and those responsible may be liable in law accordingly.

'Extreme Horror' is a work of fiction. Names, characters, businesses, organizations, places, events, and incidents either are the product of the author's imagination or are used fictitiously. Any resemblance to actual persons, living or dead, events, or locales is entirely coincidental.

For more information about the author, please visit www.mattshawpublications.co.uk

For more information about Matt Shaw, please visit
www.facebook.com/mattshawpublications

MATT SHAW PRESENTS

EXTREME HORROR

By
Matt Shaw

Starring

Michelle Prideaux

Also featuring

Barry Rowlands   Nancy Loudin

Angela Mcbride   Rhett Poore

Tara Tannenbaum   Rebecca Thompson

Sophie Hall   Gina Jones

Debra Bergevin   Colleen Cassidy

Sandra Dawson   Dawn Moore

Kirsty Forster Lee-Ann Paris

Kathryn Rock Christine Feldon

Sarah Bullen   Angela Gillmore

Henry Knoche   Rebecca Lee

Lauriette Hutzler Jennifer Kampfschulte

Debbie Dale   Carmen Brooks

Cheryl Hamilton   Jennifer Pelfrey

and

Dawn Cano

WARNING

I have had numerous one star reviews complaining that my black cover books are sick or too disgusting. I have even had people verbally attacking me in reviews - and via social media - because my work is dark and that clearly I have mental issues. None of that is a problem. I understand that it comes with the territory despite the fact that I label my work with clear warnings in order to try and put off people who are sensitive to dark subject matter. Even so... I feel I really need to stress yet another warning for this particular title.

This book is disturbing and *wrong* in places. There are some extreme scenes and there is strong language. If you are easily upset, offended, shocked, disturbed or have triggers that can set off episodes - please, please do not purchase this book. This is not a marketing gimmick. I would rather you saved your money (and your mind) by choosing something else.

Still here? 'Enjoy' the story and - remember - I *fucking warned you*.

Kind Regards,

Matt Shaw

Chapter One

A Number's Game

My numbers are not exact. I tried my best to pay attention to the films in order to keep track but I have seen them so many times now and - occasionally - my attention has been captured by something else, such as my cat meowing for attention. I believe my numbers are close though. I am also aware that there are other people who can be included in this but - to be honest - I don't really count any of the other creations as being interesting enough to warrant being on this list. They are merely cheap imitations of the following names (whom I do respect): Jason Voorhees, Michael Myers and Freddy Krueger.

It doesn't matter who I prefer from the aforementioned names but to appease your curiosity I can confirm that Freddy Krueger is my preferred *monster*. It's just a shame then that I found Robert Englund, the man who plays the monster, such a complete and utter asshole when I met him at a convention where I had waited in a long line just to get his autograph. Now, I am told he is usually a nice man. He likes to spend time chatting with his friends. He likes to pose for photographs with them despite a sign behind his seat stating no such photos can take place. I guess I got him on a bad day and I can understand why. There was, after all, a lady queuing in front of me who approached him in a negative, rude manner.

'I don't like your work but can you sign all of these for my friends?' and then the ignorant bitch proceeded to hand him a pile of photos to sign. She didn't engage in conversation as he patiently scribbled his way through the many pictures. If someone had said that they weren't a fan of mine, I guess I would be in a bad mood too but, even so… He didn't have to take it out on me.

'You're the only film boogie-man to scare the crap out of me when I was growing up,' I told him. He didn't say a word. He didn't look at me. He didn't acknowledge me. He simply signed the picture I had taken to him, handed it back and looked behind me for the next person he had to sign for. I walked away feeling devastated; my childhood hero had crushed me.

'You were just unlucky by the sounds of it,' people told me when I explained what happened. This didn't make me feel any better. If anything, it made me feel worse. Of all the shitty luck, I get him when he is pissed at some idiot who offended him in the queue before me. I wish I knew where she lived. Had I done so, she could have been my number one.

Anyway, forgive me, I have gone off on a tangent. I'm not here to discuss the actors. I am here to discuss the characters. Jason, Freddy and Michael. If you want to be pedantic about it, I'm not even here to talk about the characters. I'm here to talk about their kills. Not the specific kills - of which there are many - but rather the *number* and remember… My numbers are not exact but they are pretty damn close, I believe.

Of all the films Jason has starred in, he has so far killed approximately one hundred and forty-six people. He is the leader in the numbers game with Michael running second. He has killed ninety-four people, or thereabouts, in his films whereas Freddy has only managed about thirty-five across his films. This number is disappointing considering Freddy is my favourite of the three. It doesn't even matter that he has starred in less films. If you number crunch and look at averages, Freddy still comes out bottom of the list of killers. I'll be honest, it is a dream of mine to bring Freddy back to the big screen and - when I do - I'll ensure he charges to the front of the kill list. I'll make Freddy number one, where he belongs. Although, as a fuck you to Robert, I'd most likely use another actor unless I see him at another convention and get to see that he was just having an off day and I got the brunt of it.

Nicolas Cage. I'd make him Freddy. He can clearly do psychotic characters well and I believe he can carry Freddy's dark sense of humour too. I mean, Nic is one hell of a funny fuck. Did you ever see *The Wicker Man* remake. Comedy gold, right there ladies and gentlemen.

Back on track. Like I said, I know there are other *monsters* - for want of a better word - but I find them insignificant compared to these three. Pinhead is so-so, with pretty shitty films, Leatherface is good but let down by the sequels and the fact that, actually, he isn't the worst thing in the film - the whole damned family is fucked-up. Candyman has a good outing for his first and second film but... Just seems like *another* slasher bad guy without bringing anything new to the genre that hasn't been seen before. And, even if you do put him up there with the other three, his kills are nowhere near the same number so he isn't worth mentioning.

Believe it or not, these guys aren't actually my favourite kind of movie monster. Of the three, I stand by what I previously said with regards to Freddy being the best one but I actually prefer my murderers in films to be more realistic. The Freddy films, Jason and Michael movies too, they're fun but unrealistic. You certainly can't watch them for inspiration as to how best go on a killing spree. You start running around with knives for fingers, or clutching a large knife or machete, and the cops are going to shoot you down pretty fast. Hell, these days, you look at a cop funny and they'll shoot you regardless of whether you have a weapon or not.

As I mentioned, I prefer my monsters to be realistic. I prefer them to be the kind of person who could actually be living amongst us. You see, we all know monsters aren't real. But people like Norman Bates from *Psycho* - well we know they exist. Hell, Bates himself was created using infamous murderer Ed Gein as inspiration; some crazy fuck who liked to dress up like his mother and dig up dead people whilst trying to bring them back to life. Sound familiar? Norman Bates, based on *Psycho*. Buffalo Bill, from *Silence of the Lambs,* based on the same man. The family in *The Texas Chainsaw Massacre* - yep - part based on Gein. He would create furniture from bones, just as the family in that film did. With regards to my own work - well - I use the serial killer Damon Benton (real name Arthur J. Hopkins) as my inspiration.

When you watch my films - the ones my family said I would never be able to make - you will feel scared and uncomfortable because you know these murderers do exist. Not only are they based on real-life murderers but… Well… This isn't special effects. I am *actually* killing people and - looping back to Freddy and co. - I am gunning for their numbers.

My films will have the scariest monster, the one you can pass in a street and not recognise, *and* it will have the most kills. And the violence and creativity… It will have the most of those too. In essence; this is Extreme Horror.

Still - don't take my word for it - let me show you an example.

And with that…

I signed the white sheet of A4 paper that was now filled with my statistics and facts. My name under the words "Kind Regards and Murderous Intentions". I did not include a return address. Job done, I folded the sheet of paper in two with gloved hands before sliding it into a C5-sized envelope. I didn't seal the envelope yet. Instead I reached for the DVD on the kitchen counter and dropped that into the envelope too. It's in narrow case so it's protected from scratches that might stop it from playing properly. And it *does* play properly; I have tested it numerous times. I had to. There would be nothing more pathetic and embarrassing than sending this letter off with a faulty disk.

I would look a right dick.

I sealed the pre-stamped envelope. It's not very heavy yet I had stuck it with six self-adhesive first class stamps. It is wasteful, I know, but I don't want the hassle of going to the Post Office to get it weighed. At least I know it will definitely get to them like this. Better to have too much postage than not enough - especially as, at this stage, I am only sending out one DVD.

Last thing I want to happen is for it to get lost in the post because I didn't put the correct postage on it. Or the address…

Which reminds me.

I leaned across to my laptop and pressed the space key. The black screen lit up, illuminating the otherwise dull room with its brightness. The system was already loaded up to the television station's address page which I had been looking at earlier. A quick cross-check and I had definitely written it properly. Now, before I go to the post box at the end of the road, I just need to take a moment to really consider what I am about to do. Once this DVD gets out there, once people see it - there will be no turning back. I will soon become a household name. I'll be just as famous as Art, or Arthur as he is sometimes called, the only difference between me and him being that I won't have my freedom taken away from me. I won't be as cocksure, or stupid, as he was. I shall keep my distance… If I even go ahead and post the DVD, that is.

I looked at the envelope. It would be a shame for it to remain unseen. It really is rather good, even if I do say so myself. And just like that my mind was made up. The DVD would definitely get posted and the News station will get their introduction to me - and my work. And what an introduction it is and thanks to the spare DVD already loaded into the player… It's not only a great introduction for them, it can be a good introduction for you too. To my work at least. For the man behind the film, you'll need to stay with me. You'll need to come on this journey with me and discover more as I share the director's notes.

I reached forward to the universal remote control and aimed it across the room towards the television set. A small set with the DVD player built in underneath the screen. I pressed play and sat back.

'The Lawnmower Man'

1. EXT. FIELD - LATE

Grainy footage looking down at a lawnmower. Due to the nature of the shot, there is nothing else visible but the top of the lawnmower's main body. The shot is lit with a single, battery-powered lamp which remains out of shot.

ADAM (VOICE-OVER)

'I was twelve years old when I first watched *The Lawnmower Man*. If you look it up on the International Movie Data Base the quick outline of the film states "a simple man is turned into a genius through the application of computer science". I am in my mid-thirties now and whilst the quick description rings some bells in the back of my mind, I can't remember much about the film other than the fact that it starred Pierce Brosnan and that I was bitterly disappointed by the distinct lack of violent lawnmower scenes.'

VICTIM (OUT OF SHOT)

Please don't do this. Whatever you want. I'll get it for you, I'll do it. Anything.

(a beat)

Please, I have a family.

ADAM (VOICE-OVER)

If you want violent lawnmower scenes - as I had when I first asked my mother to rent the film for me, as I was too young to get it without her aid - you need to track down a copy of Peter

Jackson's *Braindead*. There was one scene in that film where the lead character kicks a front door in, shouts some quip and then storms into the zombie-filled house with his lawnmower raised in the air; blood and guts and limbs everywhere. It was cinematic perfection for the gore hungry child that I was and I can still picture the scene vividly, playing it back in my mind whenever the mood suits. Hard to believe that very same director then decided to go mainstream with *The Lord of the Rings* before completely fucking up *The Hobbit*. Someone needs to recreate the infamous lawnmower party scene with Jackson standing at the front of the soon-to-be-hacked crowd.

We can hear that the second man - the VICTIM - is weeping. The camera angle changes to a side-view; still a close-up of the lawnmower. As we pull away, we see that it is resting on a MAN'S face. There is a metal croquet 'gate' around his neck, digging into the ground keeping his head pinned in one place. The MAN - named RHETT POORE - is crying, clearly terrified. This is either Oscar-winning acting or very, very real.

The camera angle changes to a close-up of the start switch for the lawnmower. The shot is still, set up on a tripod. The start switch consists of a button on the handle and a safety lever. To start this particular machine, the lever needs to be squeezed and then the button pressed.

                    ADAM (CONTINUED)

Have you seen Quentin Tarantino's *Reservoir Dogs*? I watched that film when I was about fifteen years old, sixteen at a push. I wasn't actually that bothered about seeing it because the title put me off but people started saying how shocking it was. Not sure what they were watching but I wasn't shocked by anything although there was one scene that did stick in my head. Mr.

Blonde cuts the ear off a cop to the song *Stuck in the Middle with you*. I can't hear that song without thinking of that scene. I want my scene to be as powerful and long-lasting. I want people to look at lawnmowers and instantly remember what happens next; always replaying it in their mind.

(a beat)

You should be happy. You're going to be remembered forever.

ADAM'S hand squeezed the lawnmower trigger. His second hand entered the shot and hovered over the button despite the screaming from underneath the garden machinery. The camera angle changes to a side-view. We can see RHETT beneath the mower for the first time. The machine is angled so that it is resting over his face. He is screaming. The machine roars to life and RHETT screams for the split second it takes the rotary blades to slice down the length of his nose until it is nothing, before slicing into his actual face. His lips are ripped off, his skin is shredded, eye-balls burst as the sharp blades make short work of his skin, tissue and - soon enough - skull. The lawnmower isn't switched off until it is completely flat against the grass. Rhett's head is no longer there. Left behind is nothing but a mushy, minced puddle of skin, brain and bone fragment. The lawnmower engine cuts out and the blades slow to a stop. The camera stays on the image for a second longer before…

FADE TO BLACK:

Credits roll on the screen. With the exception of the VICTIM'S NAME (Rhett Poore) all names are the same; ADAM. Cameraman, editor, director, writer.

Chapter Two

Introductions and Influences

The DVD cut out and the television screen went black. Despite the temptation to watch it again, I pointed the controller once again and switched the unit off. A red light appeared on the television showing that it was in stand-by mode.

So - anyway - there you have it. That is the same film I will be sending off to the News Stations. On their DVD they have two options to watch. It autoplays on the first version - the uncut edition that I insist they see first - and then it goes to a title screen offering a pixilated version of the same film; a safer copy that can be broadcast on the television. Of course, as time goes on, I will also be uploading the films to the Internet. At the moment I'm not sure how. Or rather, I'm not sure how to upload it without it being traced straight back to me.

The more eagle-eyed viewers will notice I didn't include my surname in the film either. Truth be told, I didn't even include my first name. Adam is not my name. It is a name I gave myself. The intention being to reveal my real name on my death bed, or when I am caught just like Arthur J. Hopkins did.

Most know Arthur - or Art as he prefers to be known - as Damon Benton but that was just a name he used to keep himself hidden from the real world until he was ready for them to know who he really was. It annoys me when people talk about him and get his name wrong, calling him Damon. It feels as though they're denying him his real existence and when conversations do arise about his work, and I hear people use the wrong name, I am quick to correct them. I do not inform them that I am in communications with him, though, swapping letters; a very polite pen-pal. The very first of his letters, I can still recite word for word perfectly. I've read it so many times.

Dear Adam,

I'm glad you enjoyed my work and that you were able to find some photographs of it that remain unedited by the media, too afraid to show it in all of its gory glory. It means a lot to me to know that I have inspired you to become creative in your own chosen art-form. Too many of our children have their dreams crushed by overbearing parents who push them into careers they do not wish to be in. I should know, I was one of those very children so - really - it does mean the world to me to hear that you've decided to pick up your art once more.

I hope that your work takes you places and reaches the audience you're intending to play to. With any luck, the path you choose won't end with you moving in next door to me although - if that were to be the case - at least we would both have someone to talk to with common interests whilst we serve out our time. Lord knows my current neighbour has no vision for creativity or brains for the arts - only eyes for children. But then, I suppose that is to be expected for it is a sick world we share.

Once again, thank you for taking the time to write to me and I wish you well and - please - do keep in touch with regards to your progress.

Kind Regards,

Art.

Arthur said he was glad I had got inspiration from him to start practising my own art once more. In truth, I never lost my vision or passion for it. I was just concentrating in the wrong areas and pushing in the wrong direction; a direction which would lead to nothing but frustration and rejection letters.

I was penning screenplays and sending them off to agents and film companies. Most ignored me and the ones who didn't merely said my idea wasn't what they were currently looking for. A useless statement that offered no suggestion as to what they were seeking. It was a "thank you but no thank you" style letter and another door closed in my face.

Art made sculptures from human remains. He had always liked to make things and paint but his work never got him the recognition he deserved until he branched out, using the people he snatched from the streets; the young girl, the fat lady, even the wife of the Detective hunting him. As soon as he opened his art gallery to the general public, he became famous overnight. People seemed to go crazy for his work and there was even a bidding war on the crime scene photographs on eBay until the listing was removed. A pity considering I was winning. He had definitely hit the big-time though with a book about his life even being written by Matt Shaw and Michael Bray; one writing through the viewpoint of Art and the other writing through the viewpoint of Detective Andrews.

I read it, even told Art that I had, and I must confess to enjoying it. I liked that it didn't just try and paint him into a stereotypical monster. He had layers. I also liked the fact that the two authors didn't try and give it a shitty Hollywood Happy Ending.

I like Arthur because he had a vision and a passion for creating that I can relate to. Just like Freddy Kruegar from *Nightmare on Elm Street* he might not have had the most kills out of all the UK's serial killers but he certainly had the most memorable. I mean - come on - Sutcliffe hit people with a hammer. Anyone can do that. Art… He turned the deaths into a thing of beauty. Who remembers a girl with a dent in her head? No one other than the family, and most like y

Sutcliffe as he masturbates himself to sleep every night. Who remembers a dead mother nursing an unborn baby that had been plucked from her stomach? Everyone.

Over the months I have tried to get a visiting order to see Art in person. I want to shake him by the hand and - if permitted - take a selfie with him that I could include in the final frame of my last movie when I am ready to release it. Not only do people get to see who I am but they get to see who I am friends with but during one particularly paranoid moment I must confess to thinking the visitation orders were being refused by Art personally. Perhaps he was worried I was trying to get famous by using him? Maybe he thought I was trying to get a story out of him to sell to the press like a dirty kiss and tell? The more I thought about it the more I doubted that to be the case though. He doesn't seem to be that sort of person and besides, with less people talking about him over the last few months, he'd probably welcome the attention a story would provide. Regardless, it is a pity he can't see my work for himself, so he could know that I am talented with or without him. If only he could sit down and watch one of my films, he would see that I am just as good as he is - if not better. There would be no doubt in his head that my friendship with him is genuine. Still - no sense stressing over it. Not when I have films to make!

I started making films back at secondary school. I was about fourteen years old and one of the oldest in my group, not that I acted like it. My temper used to be quick to flare up and I'll put my hand up to admitting I could act like a spoiled brat occasionally when making my movies with the limited friends I had. An example of my temper was caught on camera once when we were filming a fight scene. My friend had frustrated me because he kept trying to change the script we were filming before every scene. He was trying to turn his character into the hero of the piece and yet that was my role. When we came to get the cameras rolling, I hit him for real - bloodying his nose with a hard, clenched fist directly to the tip. It was the last time I made a film with him although - occasionally - my other friends would still come over and continued to do so until we went our separate ways after our end of year exams.

I do not miss them.

Despite struggling to make any real friends at college, I never lost the dream of becoming a filmmaker. I used to spend hours sitting at home writing screenplays even though I had no one to film them with and - even if that hadn't been the case - no money for the budget. Neither did I have a clue as to where I could send them although that changed upon the purchasing of *The Writers and Artists Year Book*, a handy directory of producers, publishers and agents. I can't tell you how many letters I posted off, with various ideas attached, and I can't tell you how many rejections I had returned to me; rejections that were stored in a large lever arch file which I - somehow - subsequently lost.

Most people would have been put off after receiving so many "fuck offs" in the post but I wasn't. Their lack of faith in my work never bothered me but the same couldn't have been said about my mother and father lacking belief in me. I mean - who doesn't want the approval of their mum and dad? Not only did I not get the approval but they even tried to actively discourage me.

'My Life'

1. INT. OFFICE - LATE AFTERNOON

A YOUNG ADAM sits in a large, plush office. Sitting opposite him is a smartly-dressed business man - his FATHER. His name is BARRY ROWLANDS. Between them - always between them - is a large polished desk covered in a mountain of work and a noisy laptop displaying month-end figures. BARRY isn't paying any attention to what is on his desk, instead he is staring at an end of term report that he is holding in his hands. YOUNG ADAM, aged at around fifteen years old, looks rather nervous as he watches his father's face react to what he is reading.

YOUNG ADAM

Film studies was good. Mr. Jones said I was only a little way off from an 'A'. He gave me a few hints and tips as to what I could do to try and improve myself over the holidays. Told me to watch more films and pay close attention to camera angles used during particular scenes; one example he mentioned being the shower scene in *Psycho*. Did you know, you never actually see the knife penetrate the woman?

He stops talking when he realises his father is paying him no attention whatsoever.

FATHER

You're failing maths?

YOUNG ADAM

I'm struggling with maths.

FATHER

Hmmm.

YOUNG ADAM

But - you know - don't need maths to be a filmmaker.

FATHER

(Suddenly angry)

You need to get this filmmaker nonsense out of your head and get yourself a realistic goal. The film industry is one of the most incestuous businesses there is with most people only making it because of family connections. Those with no family connections are just damned lucky. That is not you. You want to write? Fine. Be an English teacher. You want to act? Not a problem - be a Theatre Studies teacher. It's low wage but at least it is a career. Get this idea of moving to Hollywood out of your head. You are not Quentin Tarantula…

YOUNG ADAM

(Correcting him)

Tarantino.

BARRY stops talking for a split second and looks at his disappointment of a son. He had wanted him to follow in his footsteps, maybe one day take over the family business when he was ready to retire. He didn't know where he had got the film-making idea from but he hated it and shot him down every time he dared mention it out loud.

FATHER

Next year you're going to drop Film Studies. There's an accountancy course that I think will suit you better. It's about time you got comfortable with numbers… Yes… I'll phone them tomorrow and get you a placement at your school. That will suit me better… It'll be good for you to get your head out of the clouds with all of this film nonsense…

YOUNG ADAM doesn't say anything but it is clear from his face that he isn't happy. The screen suddenly flashes white and YOUNG ADAM sits up quickly and snatches the letter opener from a small pot on the desk. Before BARRY has a chance to react, his son slashes angrily at his throat causing a jettison of blood to spray out and over his son. The father's eyes go wild with fear and panic as he clutches at his throat. YOUNG ADAM doesn't stop there though and climbs up on the desk and starts repeatedly stabbing BARRY with the same letter opener. The screen flashes white and everything is back to normal. The father wasn't stabbed, the son hasn't moved. We close in on YOUNG ADAM'S face and it is clear he isn't happy with what he is being told.

FADE TO BLACK

Chapter Three

My Audience

I was momentarily lost in the memory of sitting opposite my strict father in his office. Blinking excessively as my dry eyes itched, I snapped back to the present and laughed at how easily I had been side-tracked.

The amount of times I had imagined killing both him and my mother, Gina Jones. Different surnames due to the fact they divorced when I was in my twenties and my mother went back to using her maiden name. I had cut their throats wide open and danced in a rain of blood. I'd toasted marshmallows as their restrained corpses continued to twitch with petrol-fuelled fires licking at their flesh. I had danced *The Funky Chicken* as they did their own merry jig at the end of the ropes tied around their necks. I had turned the tunes up on the car radio as I slowly backed over their bodies, having already run them down; no station going loud enough to drown out the sound of bones cracking and splintering under the weight of the car. I had even poured myself more breakfast cereal as they choked to death, spitting up saliva and frothy claret along with remnants of their poisoned porridge. I had done it all and - yet - in truth I have done none of it. They continue to live on. Will they star in a film of their own one day, written by me and directed by me? Who knows. All I know is that now is not the time. Now is the time for the obligatory sex scene that all good stories need.

'Why are you telling me all of this?' my audience - and date - for the night asked. A pretty girl named Rebecca Thompson. Of course she didn't introduce herself to me as Ms. Thompson. Not even Rebecca. She introduced herself to me as *Honey* of all things. A stereotypical name for a stereotypical whore with a stereotypical story in which she works the streets to fund her addiction. Track marks on her arm gave her away yet she must be new to her unhealthy tastes for she doesn't have the wasted appearance of most drug addicts that I've come (and cum) across.

There is a panic in her wet eyes that I find a sexual turn-on. So much so, in fact, that the camera films her in extreme close-up so as to capture that very look so I never have the chance to forget it when I am older and my memory starts to fail me.

Rebecca is tied to the dining room chair, sitting at the table, at the other end of the living room which, due to space issues, I've set up as a make-shift dining room. It isn't ideal but it is better than nothing and - besides - I didn't need a living room that big. It would have just been wasted space. I have been telling her who I am and showing her my films. She is my date for the evening, she is my play-thing, she is my actress but before any of that - she is my test audience and a good one at that for she gagged when she watched *The Lawnmower Man*.

I ate my meal but she has not touched hers. She spent most of the meal screaming at me to let her go. Funny - especially given the fact I cooked her a supermarket's own brand of microwave meal - she reminded me of Vanessa from Matt Shaw's *Happy Ever After*. I actually felt a little disappointed that I hadn't realised this before setting the scene up. Had I done so, I could have put her in a sexy red PVC dress like the one Vanessa was forced into. Instead she is still wearing the clothes I picked her up in; a tiny skirt, some knee length boots and a small top. It's a slutty look let down by the fact that the clothes have seen better days - no doubt purchased from a cheap clothes store in town - and I'm sure there is dried jizz splashed on her skirt from one previous punter.

She asked again, 'Why are you telling me all of this?'

I shrugged. I don't know why I was telling her all about my life. I guess I was trying to justify my film and give her some understanding as to how it came to be. I don't know, I guess she would be more impressed if she knew the whole story about it; everything I had been through to get here. Fuck knows why. It doesn't matter what she thinks so long as she is disgusted by the video, I'm cool. She's going to die either way. Eventually. I mean - we all die sooner or later.

'Can I go home now?' she asked, her voice wavering.

I shook my head, 'We're not done yet.'

The welled up tears started to trickle from her eyes. I glanced at the whirring camera hoping that it was capturing all of this. 'What do you want from me?' she asked.

'Well that's obvious, isn't it?' I looked at her. 'Why else do men visit…' Shit, what's the correct term? Do I call them prostitutes or whores or people or ladies or… 'You?' I finished the sentence before stringing it all together for her, 'Why else do men visit you?' I moved across the room and sat opposite her at the table. Unlike my date, I had cleared my plate. 'We need to have sex,' I answered her question once more.

'And then? And then you'll let me go, yeah?'

'Sure. If you like.' I reached for the camera and pulled it from the tripod. Aiming it towards her with a nice handheld shot I gave her some necessary direction, 'Tell me you want to fuck me.'

'I want to fuck you,' she whimpered.

I shook my head, 'No. Try inviting me upstairs.'

'Do you want to go upstairs?'

I looked at her over the top of the camera. Pretty disappointing. I expected more for her.

'You're a whore,' I reminded her, 'you're supposed to be able to seduce men into sleeping with you. I mean - at the moment - if I walked past you in the street, I wouldn't look twice at you.

Most men would be the same. There are so many girls out there, working the streets, we have choices and, well, you'd be at the bottom of the choice pile of slags, you know? So clearly there must be something about you. Something that can tempt me to stick it in you… So what is it? Eyes? Are you able to turn your eyes on to make us want to believe in you?' I leaned forward and sniffed the air around her, 'It's not your perfume. What is that? Eau de Skank?'

'I'm scared.'

'Some men, believe it not, are scared when they come and see you yet they manage to hide it. Come on… Make me believe you actually want to fuck me. Make the audience believe.' I found myself getting more frustrated with her as she continued whimpering pathetically, 'A sex scene is just laughable if there is no chemistry between the actors.' I suddenly shouted, 'MAKE ME FUCKING BELIEVE IN YOU!'

She inhaled sharply and wiped her eyes with her hands before looking directly at the camera. There is a sudden sparkle - for want of a better word - in her eyes as she also pushes forward with her chest, thrusting her breasts forward. This is it. This is the whore I thought I had booked. I smiled from behind the camera as she pouted with her lips, 'I'm going to take you upstairs now and I'm going to suck your cock so hard you're going to want to shoot your thick cream straight down the back of my throat. Question is: Can you hold off long enough to fuck my arse?' She raised a teasing eyebrow.

I stopped the camera and gently lowered it. God damn. She even managed to give me a twitch down there. I looked at her with a beaming grin, 'That's what I'm talking about.' I fished in my pocket and pulled out the key to the silver cuffs keeping her on the chair. Holding them up I asked her, 'Want to go and make a movie?'

'And then you'll let me go?'

I smiled at her, 'So long as you don't try anything funny - of course.' I reassured her, 'I never wanted to hurt you. I only wanted to make a film with you. You help me… I'll let you go.' I looked for a response from her, 'Fair?'

She nodded at me slowly. Still, clearly, unsure. I guess, considering where she comes from, it's easy to see why she struggles to trust me. Doing what she does, she lines herself up to see the scum of the world; dirty fuckers crawling the curbs looking for women to abuse. It's not a nice world but - on the plus side for her at least - she'll be free from it soon enough, not that she knows this yet. No sense ruining what could be a great sex scene.

'Super 8 (inches)'

1. INT. BEDROOM - LATE EVENING

The following shots are in graphic detail. The film being made is not that of a mainstream Hollywood picture but rather an underground pornographic film of explicit content. There is little plot other than the "plot" that had been set up in the earlier living room scene where the WHORE invited the CLIENT up to the bedroom in order to suck his cock.

The first shot is a close-up of a hard penis pushing into a tight cunt and coming back out once more. A steady, rhythmic thrusting motion with male groans heard from behind the camera. The skin of the cock glistens from the clear wetness that it is coated in. There is no rubber in sight. The thrusting stops as the erection is pulled out leaving the vagina's moist opening to gape for a second or two before the penis slides back in and the thrusting starts once more.

The camera angle changes: A hand on a naked breast, squeezing it with the fingers paying particular attention to the hardened nipples. With the way the body jolts, it's obvious the penetration is still taking place. The camera shakes where it is held in the CLIENT'S other hand.

> CLIENT (out of shot)
>
> (breathing heavily)
>
> You feel so fucking amazing.
>
> (a beat)
>
> Let me taste you…

The camera angle changes: a close-up of the WHORE'S pussy lips. Glistening in the dim light from either lube, spit or her own wetness. The shot is still and steady - filmed from a tripod at a bird-eye's view. The CLIENT'S head comes into the shot and his tongue pushes deep into the WHORE'S cunt. We can hear the sound of his tongue lapping away at the vagina, pushing inside the WHORE as deep as he can get it.

The camera angle changes: a close-up of the CLIENT'S cock as he frantically jerks it whilst licking the juices from the WHORE. A "fap-fap-fap" sound.

The camera angle changes: back to between the WHORE'S legs from the WHORE'S own point of view. The CLIENT has his face buried between her legs as he continues eating her out. One of his hands is stretched up to her breast, squeezing it hard. His other hand is reaching down - stroking himself hard. The CLIENT looks up, lust in his eyes.

CLIENT

You taste fucking amazing.

As the CLIENT buries his face back between the WHORE'S legs, the camera work gets quicker and quicker - matching the level of his excitement. Close-up of his tongue inside her, his own hand stroking his erection - the tip of which is coated in pre-cum, the WHORE'S POV looking down at the scene, her fingers pushing inside her slit - working her inside with a *come hither* motion. Back to the WHORE'S POV and the CLIENT looks up at her, still tugging his cock.

CLIENT

I'm close… I want to cum on your face.

The WHORE doesn't protest and we cut to a new camera angle. We are in close-up on her face. Her skin is bruised, her throat is cut right the way across. Her mouth is open with her tongue sticking out and her eyes - glazed over - are wide open staring directly at us. From off-camera we hear the CLIENT groan and, a split second later, a string of ejaculate flies into the shot and splashes the deceased WHORE in the face.

The camera angle changes one final time: a medium shot capturing most of the room. The CLIENT is kneeling on the bed next to the dead WHORE. His cock in his hand, he has just ejaculated. He lets go of his penis and lays down next to the WHORE. He wipes the semen from her face and feeds it into the hole in her neck. He smiles to himself, finding it all rather amusing and then - just as quickly as the smile appeared - it disappears. His eyes are fixed on the slit in the WHORE'S throat. He leans close to it, overcome with curiosity, and licks it. Liking the taste, he licks it again and then for a third time as he rolls back on top of the dead girl.

FADE TO BLACK

Chapter Four

Spares

The camera continues to whirr in the corner of the bedroom where I had it set up but it's no longer filming. The film had run out some time ago but - thankfully - not before I had caught the necessary action on it.

I'm lying here with a cigarette in my mouth. I lit it a couple of minutes ago despite not actually being a smoker. Haven't taken a drag yet. Not even mine. I found it in the whore's bag

Smoking has never been my kind of thing. I tried it - once or twice - when I was younger but I didn't see what all the fuss was about. I honestly believe people who smoke are weak minded idiots who only do so because they haven't been able to kick it having once tried it when trying to look like one of the cool kids. God knows that was why I tried it. I was trying to fit in. I was trying to be cool. Instead I looked like a fool when I hacked up a lung. The people who didn't hack up a lung though, I do not believe they really enjoy it. They're simply trying to keep in with the cool kids or unable to stop themselves because of the aforementioned weakness.

I took a drag and coughed the smoke and shit back out again before stubbing the cigarette out on the dead hooker. I didn't like it back then, I don't like it now. No stress. I tossed the butt to the floor and looked back at the dead girl. It's funny how peaceful she looks despite the violent death she had gone through.

We had been sitting at the dinner table together and I had filmed the opening section of the film where she suggests we go upstairs and fuck. Initially I had been worried that I had chosen the wrong girl because - until she listened to my directions - she was dire in the role of the seductress. The second part of that scene was me leaning across, pretending to unco the restraints, and slitting her throat. A special protector over the lens of the camera stopping the blood splatter from doing any damage to the fragile components.

She never saw it coming.

It always makes me feel good to see how peaceful people look in death. Growing up, I used to be scared of it. I guess that's what you get from watching someone close to you slowly die. In this instance it was my Nan. Lung-cancer took her and it seemed as though she was suffering forever. To see the peace in their faces when my co-stars are dead... It makes me think of my Nan as being at peace. It makes me think that - no matter what comes my way - I too have peace waiting at the other end.

I could lay here all night, cuddled up next to the cold slut - soaking up the peace - but I can't. There is work to be done. Downstairs needs to be cleaned up, especially in the dining room where her blood is drying on the floor and furniture. The hooker needs to be cut up into smaller sections so I can dispose of her easier. I need to check the footage and I need to edit it together.

· With regards to the footage, it should be okay but, it's not the end of the world if it hasn't quite worked out. I had learned when I first started this game that it was good to have a back-up plan in the form of a spare co-star. In this case it's another woman that I picked up from another town whilst on business; West Yorkshire to be precise.

The identification I stole from her purse had her name listed as Michelle Prideaux. Her date of birth states she is thirty-seven but she doesn't look it. Take that as you will. Six foot tall, long curly blonde hair and hazel eyes - she's pretty enough and would make for a good sex scene. The only reason she wasn't first choice was because... Well... She isn't a prostitute.

I don't know what she does and I doubt I will get around to asking her. If the footage with the whore has come out okay I probably won't bother uttering another word to Michelle. I'll probably just storm through into the room I've restrained her in and cut her throat. Let her bleed out, cut her up and fuck her off with the other bodies that need disposing of. I won't even tell her of my plans. After all - no sense wasting breath, or time.

'Shit,' I muttered to myself. Lying here, thinking about what I need to do and thinking about what I've done isn't getting it done any sooner and I'm already tired - what with it being a long day and then me having to do all of the work in the sex scene that I filmed. Need to stop thinking things through and get on with things. Get this place tidied up so I can carry on with what needs to be done.

Make sure I am fully ready for when I send the first of the DVDs off to the press. Nothing worse than releasing something and then not having anything to back it up immediately. You get the interest of the audience only to lose it because you are forgotten about between releases. Hence my need to make more films before posting off *The Lawnmower Man*, even though the temptation to post it today is great. I must resist. Just need to be patient. It will be worth it in the end.

That's enough resting. Time to get this show on the road - starting with getting myself dressed. I climbed out of the bed and started gathering my clothes from where I'd dropped them on the floor before fucking the whore. First I stepped into my underwear and then I pulled my jeans up before throwing my shirt on. I paused a moment and looked at the naked body I'd left on the bed.

I'll start with cleaning downstairs. Just in case I fancy another crack before I dispose of the hooker. Sure I can get a couple more fucks in before she starts to smell. Could always film a little anal when I feel I can ejaculate again… I smiled to myself and left the room. Ignoring the screaming from down the landing - from the spare bedroom - I hurried down the stairs, towards the kitchen where the cleaning goods are kept.

'Okay, let's get this show on the road.'

From the Cutting Room Floor:

1. INT. SPARE BEDROOM - LATE EVENING

The room is filmed from a birds-eye view - taken from the ceiling in the corner of the room. CCTV-style footage. A WOMAN in her mid-thirties is tied to a bed. She is fully dressed. Her name is MICHELLE PRIDEAUX. Her ankles are tied to the foot of the bed via what looks to be dressing gown cords and her wrists are bound to the metal head-board with silver, heavy-duty handcuffs. No sound plays although it is obvious the terrified woman is screaming at the top of her lungs - not that this is an issue. Attached to all walls of the room is sound-proofing material.

As MICHELLE struggles with the restraints - desperate to get herself free - a clock in the bottom right of the screen shows the time. The scene starts at 10pm and plays through - in time-lapse motion - until 7am the following morning. During that time MICHELLE only slept on and off for a few hours and that was only due to both physical and mental exhaustion.

At 7:10am the door opens and ADAM walks in pushing a table with wheels into the room. On the table is the same television set that had been previously set up in the living room, the one with the built in DVD-player.

ADAM'S mouth moves as he greets MICHELLE, although - thanks to the lack of sound being recorded - we do not hear what is exactly said. He pushes the television to the far wall - opposite the bed - and plugs the power supply into the socket in the wall. He moves out of the way of the set so he doesn't block MICHELLE'S view and then pulls a remote control from his pocket. He points it at the screen and presses play.

The television screen lights up the otherwise dim room. Due to the poor quality of the CCTV camera, we do not see what is being played due to the television screen flickering violently although it is obvious that he is showing her one of his films.

Horror is etched on MICHELLE'S face whilst ADAM seems to be smiling.

Chapter Five

Constructive Criticism

I was proud of how the sex scene had played out. I had actually cut out the part where you see me kill the girl so the scene goes straight from her saying she wants to suck my cock and have me in her arse to the bedroom action itself. The fact she is dead - the whole time we fuck - comes as a plot twist at the completion of the scene. I think it's much more powerful this way and, as a result, I love it. Even so, before I got rid of my house-guest, I felt it would be a good idea to get a second opinion from a test audience.

Her initial reaction was great. She asked why I was showing her this. I didn't tell her what it was, I just told her to keep watching and let me know what she thought. She squirmed a little during the sex scene itself - before the twist, that is - although I couldn't tell if this was because she was getting turned on or because she felt uncomfortable. Her face was a little flushed so maybe the first of the two potential reasons?

As for the last reaction - the one where the twist hits home... Perfect. She was both suitably shocked and disgusted and I couldn't help but laugh. I had turned the television off again before asking her what she thought of my little film.

'Well?' I pushed her for an answer.

'You're sick!'

'Yeah I think it is fair to say this will be billed as Extreme Horror. You never know - might even title the DVDs with that when I send them off.' I laughed and laughed again when a quick thought flashed through my mind, picturing myself labelling the film with the *Disney* logo instead of the words *extreme horror;* make it more of a surprise for the potential viewers when they pop the film into their player. Imagine expecting *Bambi* and ending up with this although - to be fair - my mother didn't let me watch *Bambi* because she felt it was a horror due to the mother being killed.

Seriously? The mother being killed? She wasn't killed. They simply stopped drawing her. And, in the film, you never saw it anyway. You only heard the gunshot. For all we know, the mother lives on. She simply skipped town, fed up with looking after her kid. The gunshot was the perfect excuse for escape.

Whoops. Off on a tangent again.

'Why are you doing this?' Michelle asked me, still with a look of distaste on her face Is that aimed at me or is she picturing the film still? Hopefully the latter. Just because I create horror, does not mean I am a monster.

I wasn't going to tell her all of the little details. I didn't think it necessary at first and - truth be told - I was getting sick and tired of explaining myself every time I made someone watch one of my films. But - the more I thought about it - the more I considered doing so. If she knows my plan, if she knows what I am hoping to achieve, maybe she will be able to give me further insight as to whether I have actually put myself on the right tracks for stardom and infamy?

'I want to make films that will be remembered...'

'I watched *E.T* when I was a little girl - I still remember it and that film didn't rely on any of what you did here...'

I looked at her blankly, unsure as to whether she was trying to be funny. *E.T* is a science-fiction film and - to its credit - a very good one, even if the alien does look like a healthy turd with eyes. I'm not about science-fiction, though. I am all about the horror; my favourite genre. And the problem with horror is that there is so much of it flooded across the market with 95% of t being complete shit that is easily forgotten. I don't want to be part of that crowd. I want to be part of the 5%. I want to be remembered like the two directors behind *The Blair Witch Project* not that I can recall their names right at this particular minute. Okay, they're a bad example but the film was at least good.

I summed it up briefly for her, 'I make horror. *E.T* is a different genre.' I let that sink in for a minute before continuing, 'The problem with the horror market is, it is filled with so much shit that there is potential for the good films to be swallowed up in the black void of bollocks.' She was still looking at me blankly.

'Like any genre.'

'You don't get it.' I pointed to the DVD-player, 'The film in there will be remembered. You heard of the serial killer Arthur J. Hopkins? Or the other name he used - Damon Benton? He killed people and displayed them as his works of Art... This is the same thing. I'm creating my films with victims... They'll be remembered...'

She started laughing at me. I felt my insides start to bubble. I've never liked people mocking me. It's the quickest way to get me angry. The fastest way to make me lash out. Unless that is what she is trying to make me do? She wants me to lash out and end her life quickly; save her from becoming a victim in one of my films. I wonder if she'd still want that if I showed her one of my out-takes? A little film I was making with Angela McBride. I had had so many plans for that woman but she started mouthing off at me instead of screaming. She was calling me names and saying how pathetic I was, over and over again and - well - I snapped. I hit her repeatedly in the face with a clenched fist. Even when she went quiet and stopped moving, I didn't stop. Just kept hitting her until my knuckles were all split open and I couldn't tell if my hands were coated in my blood or hers. When I did finally stop, her face was flat and didn't resemble anything human. A piece of tooth had snapped away and imbedded itself in my still clenched fist… I pushed the satisfying thoughts to the back of my head and took a deep breath. This woman will not get the better of me.

'What's so funny?' I asked her.

'You're pathetic.'

'I'm sorry?'

'You're a copycat. That's what you'll be remembered for - if you're even remembered. This has been done. You said it yourself, Damon…'

'Arthur,' I snappily corrected her as my face flushed.

She continued regardless, 'He's done this already. He killed people, he made them part of his so-called art and now you're doing the same. People won't remember you and if they do - it will be as the sick fucker who copied the serial killer.' She laughed again, 'In fact… It gets worse. There was another person in the news about a year ago…'

'What are you fucking talking about?'

The way she was laughing at me, the way she found this so fucking amusing… I glanced up to the CCTV camera and wondered whether the quality would be good enough to pick up what I am going to do to her; save getting the proper camera out.

Keep calm, I thought.

'I can't remember his name but if you Google it…'

I snapped again, 'What the fuck are you talking about?'

'He travelled the country in his rig. He had turned the back area into a torture chamber… Apparently he killed himself and the last of his victims by setting everything alight inside.'

'That's nothing like what I am doing.'

'Except they found traces of a book where they believed he wrote parts of his crimes down.'

'You're lying.'

'Google it.'

'He set himself alight? How did the book survive?'

Michelle snapped suddenly, 'Why the fuck would I lie, you piece of shit? It's not like it's going to do me any good, is it?'

That was true. Whatever happens next, even before this conversation, she's going to die. I'll be honest though, she's most likely going to die a hell of a lot worse now than the way I would have disposed of her before. What can I say? She's annoyed me. But what she is saying - is she right? Am I not original enough to be remembered? Thinking back to when Arthur was in the press, there was no one else like it at the time. He was the worst serial killer for as long as I could remember. The media spoke of him for months. Will they do the same for me or will I be a flash in the pan?

My mind drifted to *The Blair Witch Project* once more. At the time it was one of the first found footage style films. Since its release - and, of course, success - it has spawned countless films copying its style. They copy it and yet come nowhere near matching its success. In fact, despite knowing I have seen so many found footage style films, I can't remember the name of any of them. Will my story be the same? A flash in the pan with headlines making more reference to Arthur J. Hopkins than to me?

She's looking at me, expecting an answer from me but I have no idea what to say to her. I need to know if this truck driver killer is real or whether she is trying to throw me off balance. It will be bad enough if people think I am copying one serial killer but two? I don't want to be a copycat. Copycats are insignificant.

I cleared my throat and made an excuse to walk out of the room so I could go and investigate her claims, 'I have to return some video-tapes,' I told her. It was the first thing that came into my mind for some reason. It wasn't until I left the room that I realised why. In the film *American Psycho*, Patrick Bateman breaks up with his girlfriend in a restaurant. She makes a scene, crying like a pathetic shit and - embarrassed - he makes an excuse to leave her there. Yep. He had to return some fucking video-tapes.

Considering the mood I started the day in - despite the lack of sleep - it certainly is taking a shitty turn. As I make my way down the stairs to where my laptop is stashed underneath the glass coffee table in the living room, I just hope what she is saying isn't true. And - if it is - I hope there is a way of salvaging all that I have done so far.

'Melting Away'

1. INT. GARAGE - LATE AFTERNOON

It is a typical double-garage. There is a car parked on one side of the garage. The bonnet is up and the engine is clearly in a state of disrepair. Along the back of the wall are all the tools you can imagine to find in a garage; hammers, boxes of screws and nails, drills, drill bits, sledge hammer, chainsaw, garden tools etc.

The camera looks at all of the tools and then to the car before panning around to a man who is tied to a chair. He will be known as VICTIM, just as they all are, but his real name is HENRY KNOCHE. In time, though, that will be forgotten - just as all of the other victims will also be forgotten with the exception of their deaths. No one will forget those.

VICTIM looks to the camera. There is fear in his eyes. We move closer to him and he responds by shaking his head and mumbling through the gag that covers his mouth.

We pass straight past him - towards a tripod that's nearby - and then turn back to face him. The camera shakes for a moment as the operator attaches it to the tripod.

ADAM walks into the shot and approaches the VICTIM.

ADAM

You looked scared.

VICTIM

I don't want to die.

ADAM

You think you should be allowed to live?

VICTIM

Yes. I haven't hurt anyone, I haven't done anything.

(a beat)

I don't deserve to die.

ADAM

Okay.

VICTIM

What?

ADAM

I said "okay".

ADAM undoes the restraints binding the VICTIM to the chair. The VICTIM doesn't move. He stays on the seat, too afraid to move for fear of what will happen to him. Despite being told he can go, he doesn't trust ADAM.

                ADAM

      What are you waiting for?

               (a beat)

      Go. Before I change my mind.

              VICTIM

           That's it?

                ADAM

    Did you really think I was going to hurt you?

              VICTIM

      I just don't understand.

                ADAM

    It's a prank. Go on… Get out of here.

               (a beat)

      Oh - before you go…

ADAM walks over to the workbench. There is a mug there. He picks it up and takes it back over to the VICTIM. He goes to take a sip from it and stops himself before laughing.

			ADAM

		I'm just joking.

		(a beat - he holds the mug out to VICTIM)

		Guess you're thirsty. Have this and be on your way.

He holds the mug out to VICTIM but the VICTIM doesn't take it. He looks at it and back up to ADAM who smiles at him and nods towards the glass. The smile suddenly disappears from ADAM'S face and he throws the contents of the mug into the VICTIM'S face who proceeds to scream; a high-pitched shriek as he covers his now smoking face with his hands. ADAM is laughing and takes a step back.

The VICTIM lurches away from the chair and moves his hands away from his face. Even ADAM is shocked by what he sees - although still pleasantly pleased with the results of his handiwork. The VICTIM'S skin is red, blistering and even appearing to *leak* from the face as though sliding from his skull. He reaches out for ADAM - his hands also going the same way as his face; no doubt damaged when he raised them to his face.

			VICTIM

		(struggling to speak)

Help me…

The screen pauses. We can see the VICTIM'S injuries in grim detail. His lips are blistering, his skin oozing from his face and his eyeballs with a soggy, mushy look to them - the whites of the eyes now red and the centres now a cloudy grey. Even his ears look as though they haven't been spared and appear to be stretching unhealthily, also melting. If the screen were to be un-paused, the VICTIM'S features would continue to slide down his face until he was no longer recognisable as a human. It's a horrible death that fills ADAM'S nostrils with the stink of burning flesh mixed with the heavy scent of the chemicals he had used.

The screen stays paused.

Chapter Six

Lacking Originality

Robocop! That's what this particular scene reminds me of. Fuck sake.

I tossed the remote control across the other side of the room and didn't bat an eyelid when it smashed against the wall. I was so fucking confident about that scene and now I detest it. A wasted afternoon of filming and an equally wasted evening of cleaning - and what a load of cleaning there was with the puddles of melted skin on the floor. Truly disgusting.

That was the first DVD in the pile though. Whilst waiting for the kettle to boil for my morning cup of tea, before searching on the computer for proof Michelle wasn't lying, I thought I would watch one of my films to convince myself I'm doing the right thing by making them. Yet it has had the opposite effect. Just made me doubt myself even more; a doubt planted there by that bitch upstairs.

I stomped over to the DVD shelving unit in the corner of the room and opened the drawer that ran across the bottom of it. It is filled with DVDs in slim jewel cases. *My* film collection - stored away in the drawer with the rest of the unit overfilled with films I have purchased over the years. It's a collection of mostly horror but there are some comedy films in there too. Some of them are still sealed in their wrapping; purchased on a whim never to be watched.

Are my films destined to never be watched? More to the point, do I ever want them to be seen - if they're cheap knock-offs of films already out there in the public consciousness? Looking at the stack of home-made films I realised I'm going to have to go through them all Check all of them to see if there is any spark of originality in there. See if there is *anything* I can use moving forward.

I took the first stack of films from the drawer and set them on the coffee table before reaching back into the drawer for the next stack. So many DVDs. So many victims. It would be a shame if none of them can be used... And to think - it's all because of that bitch upstairs, making me doubt myself.

Cunt.

Positioning myself between the DVD player and the coffee table, I reached across and ejected the *Melting Away* DVD. I tossed it to the side as though it were a frisbee. It didn't shatter when it hit the wall but I doubt it will work properly again, should someone give it a try.

I grabbed the second DVD and dropped it into the player. The machine sensed the change in pressure and automatically closed and the disk span up into life. The television flickered as the picture rolled onto the screen.

'I want to play a game,' I was off-camera, talking to the lady on-screen. If memory serves correctly her name was Nancy Loudin but that is by the by. I shuddered at the opening line; a direct rip-off of the *Saw* franchise and - from that line - it only gets worse as I put the girl through her paces with a promise of freedom if she plucks her own eyes out using nothing but a fork.

I got up and moved back to the sofa without taking my eyes from the screen. There was a sense of satisfaction watching the film play out but it was short-lived knowing it was - for all intents and purposes - *Saw*.

The first eyeball plucked out of the socket and dangled there after the woman squeezed fork prongs between the ball and the skull - pushing in from the side. A loud-piercing scream as she did so that filled my heart with joy but only because I knew - to others - it would cause fear.

I pressed eject and pulled the DVD from the tray as soon as it was free enough to do so. It followed *The Melting Man* across the room - at speed - and was replaced with another film which loaded more or less immediately.

I'm in the shot, dancing in front of the camera with a smile on my face. I am naked underneath a skin suit I'm wearing - cut from the body of Kirsty Forster. My cock is tucked back between my legs not that you can tell. Thanks to the suit and the way it was cut from her body, peeled off in the same way you'd remove the skin of an apple, all you see between my legs is her vagina. A hint of bush on the pubic mound.

Of all my victims, so far, she is the only one I knew personally. A girl with the sexiest of smiles and a twinkle in her eyes that would seduce any man. A girl I had wanted to fuck. A girl who had turned me down without hesitation. A frigid bitch. The nice thing about wearing her as a suit - recalling it perfectly as I watch the film back - I get to control her. I *become her* and when I ask her to fuck me this time, she says 'yes'.

'Would you fuck me? I'd fuck me?' I asked on-screen.

My heart sank further.

In *Silence of the Lambs* Buffalo Bill dances in front of a fucking mirror, wearing a skin-suit.

I opened the player again and - for a third time - threw the disk across the room. Enough of this! I know - looking at the remaining pile - none of the films are going to satisfy me at the moment. Not until I've checked up on what Michelle had said to me. I need to know if there is any truth in what she said. I mean, it's enough of a worry that people may consider me a copy-cat of Arthur but, if I am clever, I might be able to work my way around that. But not if there was another killer acting out his fantasies and writing them down for the world to see. And especially if - on top of that - all of my films are mirroring well known releases already.

Please just let her be on the wind-up.

Please let her just have said that in a desperate attempt to buy herself more time. Either way - foolish woman. I'm going to make her suffer. Slowly.

My computer was in the far corner of the room. A tidy little machine with all the latest editing software installed but I'm not interested in those programs at the moment, just the information that is potentially available on *Google* if what that bitch says is true.

I moved across the room and sat in the leather office chair in front of the screen. The machine is on - always on. Such a pain in the arse to turn it off and have to wait for it to load whenever I wanted to use it. Easier to let it be.

Serial killer, United Kingdom, Truck, Torture chamber - a list of keyword searches. I pressed the return tab on the keyboard and took a deep breath, hoping it wouldn't list anything remotely close to what Michelle had told me. The screen changed in an instant and my heart dropped. There it was - the top result.

I followed the link and - not that I saw how it was possible - my heart sank further as I started reading. She hadn't given me much information but there was a lot more, readily available online without much searching necessary. I felt sick as I read the opening paragraph of the first page; a horror lover disheartened by the lack of decent horror terrorised the country, travelling up and down the quiet roads in his rig, the back of which had been transformed into a torture chamber. Rumour had it, he wrote down what he did in his own personal book, his very own horror novel. Traces of this were found in the burnt remains of his rig but what really happened - the atrocities he actually committed - remain a mystery due to the destruction caused by the fire. That's my one saving grace, the fact they've been able to put some of the puzzle pieces together but not all of them. Harder to sensationalise the story and push it to media when they don't know the true facts although I am surprised that stopped them. Normally the press isn't *that* bothered.

I backed out of the page, back onto *Google,* and started looking at the rest of the bits and pieces that had been written. Most articles had the same sparse information. God only knows how Michelle had found out about it. I had never heard about it and all of the information is written on small, inconsequential, sites that I've never heard of before now. Not one single article on a respected site - such as *The Daily Mail*. I laughed to myself - the thought of them being respectable.

I closed the Internet Browser and sat back unsure of how best to proceed. The serial killer might not be well documented but it's fair to say he existed and if Michelle knew about him, other people will have heard of him too. And maybe my own crimes will get *his* crimes highlighted once more? A little like the high school shootings that take place in America. If there is a new shooting, the news stations always mention the other ones that have taken place before. Sandy Hook massacre happened, shocking the world, and the reporters also mentioned what happened at Columbine High School back in the late nineties.

Will this be the same?

My videos will be discussed across the networks but - will this truck torturer be brought up too? And Arthur, we are different yet somehow the same with what we do - channeling our art with murders. Will he also be discussed? I used a fake name when writing to him in prison but… Will anyone find out? Will those letters get leaked and my friendship with him used to tarnish my originality further?

Fuck.

What a tangled web we weave. Or something like that anyway.

I span around in the chair so that I was facing away from the computer and back into the living room area. My house is feeling small now despite being an above average size for the area. Actually my whole world is feeling small. My frail confidence had slowly started to build when I first started making these films and now… Now it has been knocked again and I am feeling like a fraud.

How am I supposed to make my mark on the world when everything has already been done?

My mind skated back to *Robocop,* a much loved film originally released in the late 80s - it was re-made in 2014 and there was a massive backlash against it with people saying it had been done and that you shouldn't touch a classic.

I definitely need to re-think my plans.

Definitely.

Need a change…

'Necessary Changes'

1. EXT. BATHROOM - LATE EVENING

We walk down the landing of a house towards a closed door at the end of the corridor. We are in the POV of ADAM. A hand stretches out from behind the camera and pushes the door open when we approach it. On the other side of the door is a bathroom; illuminated by the light hanging from the ceiling. We step in and look to the left - a bathtub. Inside the tub is a woman. Her name is LEE-ANN PARIS. For screenplay purposes she shall be known as VICTIM. She sees us and screams through the gag covering her mouth.

We look towards the toilet. In front of it, a tripod stands on the floor, ready to be used. We move across and the camera angles get shaky as we are rested on the tripod. ADAM sits on the toilet (lid down) and turns the camera towards the bathtub. The tripod is positioned in such a way, we can see into the tub with ease. We can see the fear on LEE-ANN'S face.

ADAM

I understand that you're scared but you must have known this day was coming.

(a beat)

You chose to mix in those circles and - well - you have to pay the piper sooner or later.

She tries to speak through the gag. ADAM gets up and removes the gag for her, before sitting back down on the toilet once more. He doesn't say anything. He waits for her to repeat what she was trying to say - even though he already knows what is coming.

VICTIM

I had nothing to do with what he was doing.

ADAM

But you knew about it and didn't try and stop it.

VICTIM

He said he would kill me.

ADAM

You had plenty of opportunity to get away from him. You chose not to, though.

VICTIM

It wasn't that easy. He has friends.

ADAM

You expect me to believe that?

(a beat)

Well it doesn't matter now anyway. Not for you at least. The time has come to pay the price.

ADAM gets up and walks over to the bathtub. He sits on the edge of it, positioning himself so as to get both himself and LEE-ANN in the frame. We notice now that his clothes are bloody.

VICTIM

Please don't do this.

ADAM

Do what?

VICTIM

Don't kill me.

ADAM

Kill you? Why would I do that? I just want to teach you how to suck a cock properly.

VICTIM

What?

ADAM

I mean, you need to brush up on your skills. I think, if you did, he wouldn't have had to go and fuck those kids. You could have spared all of those lives he tarnished with his dirty little hobby.

VICTIM

Please. It wasn't me.

ADAM

I know it wasn't *but* you had the power to stop it and that's why you're here. You're being punished because you could have stopped it at any time. Instead you turned away from it, even when it was painfully obvious as to what was happening.

VICTIM

No.

ADAM

Anyway - we're done talking about it. I'm going to teach you how to pleasure a man. I think if you learn how to do that - and make it really good… I like to think there is no danger of this happening ever again. You know - when you meet another man…

VICTIM

You killed him?

ADAM

I didn't.

ADAM (continued)

He is alive. He just...

(a beat)

I had to...

LEE-ANN starts to panic.

VICTIM

What have you done?

ADAM

Let's not talk about her anymore.

VICTIM

Her?

ADAM

Him... Her... What does it matter?

(a beat)

ADAM (CONT.)

This is about you now. And - for your first lesson on how to please a man… I'm going to teach you how to suck a cock.

ADAM stands and undoes his trousers. LEE-ANN struggles against the restraints, hoping to break free as ADAM reaches into his underpants before pulling out a severed penis. LEE-ANN screams as she realises he has cut it from her boyfriend. ADAM reaches into the bathtub with the severed cock and shoves it in LEE-ANN'S mouth. With one hand, he holds it there. His other hand, he places over her nose preventing her from getting any air. He places all of his weight on her, as she struggles beneath him - gradually turning blue. Eventually, the struggling stops.

FADE TO BLACK

Chapter Seven

A Change of Direction

Michelle didn't say anything to me when I walked into the room. She just watched me, waiting for me to say what was on my mind. She could tell I was wired though, buzzing with excitement and barely able to contain what I wanted to say - not that that was a problem.

'A romance!' I let it slip excitedly.

'What?'

'That's what I am going to do. I'm going to make a romance.' I took a breath before continuing, 'I'm not wasting what I have already done. The horror aspect will go at the start of my story…'

'What are you talking about?' She suddenly screamed out, 'Let me the fuck go!'

I shook my head, 'I can't.' A flash of a smile, 'You're going to be the star of the piece.'

'What are you talking about?' she asked again.

'If you'll let me get a word in - I'll explain…'

'I just want to go home,' she interrupted again.

I ignored her. I just need to get this out in the open otherwise I'll never get to say it. We'll just keep going round and round in circles like a broken record, 'I'm going to turn myself in eventually… Or I am going to take my own life, I'm undecided on the exact ending but… Here's the plan. I am going to put all of the films I am creating into one long feature. The feature will start with the kills I've already done. After all, no sense wasting them… Then I'm going to kill you…' There is obvious panic on her face so I quickly continue before she starts begging me for her life, just as they always do, 'but I won't do it. You're going to tell me you know of my work and you're a fan.' I paused a moment, 'I'm not sure how you know of it - maybe one of the news stations leaked the footage before I was ready… Maybe they found a body or something. Anyway, at the moment it's not important. What's important is - you're going to tell me that you love me. You love what I do and what I stand for. You love the passion I have…'

'You're fucking crazy,' she interrupted me.

'No. No I'm not. And ssh. I'm talking.' I continued, 'You're going to convince me not to kill you and over a space of a couple of days, I start to fall for you. An unlikely friendship starts up, with you tied down the whole time, but - eventually - it blossoms into something else. We become a couple.'

'I won't do it…'

I chose to ignore her, 'And - when we're a couple - that's when I turn my back on the horrors. I find peace within myself. It's a film about pain and torture and redemption…

'You're insane.'

'I think - by the end of it - it will be pretty damned powerful. And, even though there are real murders, we'll be able to get a deal on this. It will be released in the mainstream with all of the news stations reporting on it. We'll be on the television, we'll be in the papers… We'll be remembered!'

'I don't want to be remembered! Not like that!'

'It's the only way someone like you will be remembered.' I explained further, 'Look - we have established that all horror has been covered. Whether it's in the films or in real life - it has been done. But it's never started so viciously and ended so lovingly as the way we're going to portray it.' I smiled, still excited by my new plan, 'This is going to be incredible. We can't fail and - added bonus - you get to survive and, not just that, you get a starring role in this masterpiece.

'I don't want a starring role. I don't want any role. And I certainly don't want to be remembered as someone who falls in love with a madman.' She shook her head, 'I don't care what you do - you'll have to fucking kill me. I won't do it.'

'You will. You just don't know it yet.'

'Eat shit.'

I smiled at her. 'You're obviously tired. I'm going to go downstairs to prepare you something to eat. Give you some time to think about it all. I appreciate I've just fed you a lot of information to digest in a short space of time.'

Michelle didn't say anything to me. She simply tugged again at the ropes tying her to the bed. I glanced towards the heavy-duty knots; they weren't about to come undone anytime soon. I smiled again, slightly disappointed by her reaction, and walked from the room convinced this change was the correct thing way to go. As far as I am aware there has never been a horror movie which has changed direction halfway through and become a romance. Yes. This is going to be good.

I closed the bedroom door when I stepped out onto the landing on the off chance she started screaming. I don't have any neighbours but it doesn't mean she isn't capable of bugging the shit out of me and giving me a damned headache if she were to scream.

Still - buzzing - and ready to help her change her mind - I started down the stairs in order to prepare her dinner. A hope that she enjoys what is to be on the menu before my mind started considering how best to turn the horror scenes already finished into a longer film - joined by a single narrative. Had I known it was going to go this way, before I started, there's a good chance I would have filmed them differently. And - possibly - I wouldn't have filmed so many!

Plenty of time to think about that whilst I work on Michelle. In the meantime - dinner. Down the stairs, through the corridor and into the kitchen - I grabbed a plastic container from one of the many cupboards. With any luck, this will be the perfect size.

With any luck.

Container tucked under one arm, I walked back through to the living room. I grabbed a newspaper from the coffee table with my spare hand and headed back out of the room with another thought in my mind: *Should I be filming this for the DVD's Behind the Scenes montage?* No time now - dinner is nearly ready and will ruin if I stop to set up the camera. Besides, not even sure that it is charged at the moment.

*

I pushed the bedroom door open. I thought Michelle might have been asleep but she wasn't. Her eyes were wide open and she was staring directly at me. She's wired to the max; looks as though she's had a heavy night on cocaine.

'I thought you might have been sleeping,' I told her - unsure of what else to say.

'How could I be?' she hissed.

There's such venom in her voice. She hates me and I can't help but wonder whether I'm barking up the wrong tree with this woman. Might be easier to fuck her off and pick someone else. It's not as though I struggle to find people for my films.

I changed the subject before she started shouting at me, 'I've brought your dinner.'

I held up the plastic container I was carrying in my hands.

'I'm not hungry.'

'You need to eat.'

'Fuck you.'

I sighed. When I had first seen her, she hadn't seemed as though she'd be the mouthy sort and yet... She's a tramp. A worse mouth on her than the many whores I've collected from the streets. At least with street-walkers, you expect it. Definitely a surprise picking a *normal* person up and finding them to be even more trashy.

Goes to show - you should never judge a book by the cover. My mind hopped back momentarily to the author Matt Shaw. Hard to judge a book from his cover. A distinct lack of imagination sees him mostly use plain black covers for his work. How do you judge "black"? Mind you - silly question. There are parts of America which judge black things all too quickly.

'Hang 'em high, Merl!'

'You need to eat,' I repeated myself. 'Besides, I went to a lot of trouble over this.'

'Fuck you.'

'You really do have a potty mouth. Has anyone ever told you that?'

'No one has ever tied me to a bed before,' she spat back.

'Well then,' I smiled, 'you've never lived.'

'You know what I meant.'

I walked over and sat next to her, on the bed. The container rested in my lap. I wonder if she has realised I'm wearing gloves yet. I'm all about the hygiene, me.

Realising we were getting nowhere fast, I decided to spell things out to her, 'Listen - I'm not going to kill you. You're going to help me...'

'I'm not,' she interrupted me - a bad habit she has; nearly as frustrating as a dog that continually drags its dirty arsehole across the carpets.

I ignored her and continued, 'If you don't help me I'm going to be forced to hurt you. You understand that? *Hurt* you, not *kill* you. There is a big, big difference. And - whilst I am hurting you - you're going to smile. You're going to look as though you're enjoying it. You're going to thank me and if you don't… It will just get worse for you - but I still won't kill you. I can keep this going for the rest of your life. You understand that? I can make this last years. But if you help me… We'll be done sooner. The film will be finished and I'll be ready to show my work to the general public. I won't need you anymore and you can leave.'

'I don't believe you. You won't let me go.'

'Yes. I will. You're missing the point of this film now. It's not about the horror. I've done the horror. It's about the romance. It's not very romantic if I kill you, is it?' I didn't say anything else for a moment. I let it sink in. I want this film to happen and it can't without her. I know I could get someone else but I don't want to have to explain it all to someone else. It takes too much time and it's frustrating now. I am so close to the end game, I just want to get there.

'Just let me go. Please…'

I sighed. She just doesn't get it. Well then, dinner time.

'Mouth of Madness'

1. INT. SPARE BEDROOM - MID AFTERNOON

ADAM is sitting on the edge of the bed. On his lap is the container. MICHELLE is on the bed, tied down. The scene is captured by a CCTV camera in the corner of the room. ADAM sets the container on the floor and walks from the room. MICHELLE isn't left long. ADAM comes back with a camera in his hands, along with a tripod. He sets it up close to her face - pointing the camera directly at her much to her obvious frustration.

The camera angle changes. We view the scene from the camera that has just been brought back into the room. We are in a close-up of MICHELLE'S face.

We hear the container lid open.

>   ADAM (off camera)
>
>   Open your mouth.

>   MICHELLE
>
>   (scared)
>
>   What is it?

>   ADAM
>
>   Dinner.

ADAM'S hand comes into the shot with two gloved fingers held out. On the end of the fingers is what can only be described as human excrement. MICHELLE sees it and smells it at the same time and gags; a deep retching from the stomach followed by a cough. Her eyes water from the gagging.

                        ADAM

                What's the matter? You don't like it?

                        MICHELLE

                Get the fuck away from me.

                        ADAM

                I said "open your mouth".

MICHELLE clamps her mouth shut. ADAM leans in and grabs her face with his other hand (also gloved). With heavy pressure, he forces her mouth open and shoves the dirtied fingers in - smearing them on her teeth and tongue. By the time he removes his fingers, she is coughing violently - trying not to spew - and her teeth are caked in brown, as is the area between tooth and gum.

                        ADAM

                You like that?

She cannot answer. She is too busy retching and trying to spit the mess out the corner of her mouth. ADAM clamps her mouth closed and keeps it that way until the poor woman swallows. Only then does he remove his hand from the shot. Tears are streaming down her face and remnants of a brown, sticky shit cling between her teeth. She is still gagging.

ADAM

Don't you fucking sick that back up. You do that - you have to eat whatever comes back up!

(a beat)

And you still have the rest of the dish to finish.

ADAM'S hand comes back into the shot. Again, two fingers are covered in shit. There is a piece of corn on the very tip which he find amusing.

ADAM

One of your five a day.

MICHELLE moves her head to the side and clamps her mouth closed once again. ADAM sighs and - for the second time - forces her mouth open with his spare hand. He holds the dirty fingers just in front of her mouth, smearing a bit on her lips.

ADAM

You need to make more of an effort to look like you're enjoying this. I went to a lot of trouble to make this for you.

(a beat)

ADAM (continued)

Lick your lips.

(shouts at her when she doesn't)

I said lick your fucking lips.

MICHELLE'S tongue comes out and tentatively licks her lips. The immediate response is to gag as the rotten taste and stink hits the back of her throat.

ADAM

You're going to eat this and you're going to smile and thank me. You're going to enjoy every fucking mouthful I offer you, okay? If you do - I might not make you eat the lot. If you don't...

You have to eat every last drop...

(a beat)

If you're struggling... Just pretend it is chocolate.

MICHELLE tries to speak but her mouth is still clamped shut.

ADAM

Nod if you understand me.

MICHELLE nods slowly, tears still streaming from her eyes. ADAM releases her mouth and pauses a moment with his muddied fingers still in front of her.

                              ADAM

        You don't look as though you're enjoying it. When I enjoy something, I usually smile.

                            (a beat)

                      You're not smiling.

She forces a smile. We see just how much shit is caught between her teeth now. There is a lot.

                              ADAM

                          That's better.

                            (a beat)

                  Lick my fingers. Lick them clean.

Movement on-screen changes to half-speed, a trick to be added during the post production of the scene. In slow motion, MICHELLE'S tongue unfolds from her mouth and runs up ADAM'S fingers, mostly cleaning them in the process. The brown sticky mess pasting MICHELLE'S otherwise pale pink tongue. The shit's texture is picked up perfectly in the viewfinder - lumpy and ugly looking. Camera speed returns to normal when she starts gagging. ADAM is impressed.

ADAM

Hold it down. Don't you fucking throw that shit back up. Swallow it down.

MICHELLE swallows hard and then spits a brown frothy mess from the corner of her mouth. It dribbles down her chin. Bits floating in the spit.

ADAM

(Laughing)

Probably won't tell someone to eat shit again will you?

The screen freezes on MICHELLE'S face, crap stuck between her teeth, brown frothy mess running down her chin, her skintone a slightly green hue.

FADE TO BLACK.

Chapter Eight

Stubborn to the End

Making myself some lunch and I couldn't help but gag as I spread the *Nutella* across the toasted bread. A brown smear which reminded me of Michelle and her lunch. How the hell she managed to do that without sicking it back up is beyond me. Just as well, though, I can't handle people throwing up. Even when she gagged, I had to concentrate not to gag myself.

I looked at the plate, the toast, the brown sticky mess covering it and - without any hesitation - pushed it all to one side, closer to the sink. I have no idea why I thought I was hungry for *Nutella*. That was never going to be a good idea. I suppose chocolate is ruined for me now too. I'll always think of her tongue scraping up my fingers collecting the shit. And I'll never be able to forget how it had looked plastered between her teeth. Jesus, I'd hate to have to floss that out of there. Dental floss smells bad enough as it is once coated in the day's food.

That's it. Definitely not hungry now.

It's funny when you really think about it. I was disgusted by what I had just put Michelle through, and put off my dinner and yet once - I had opened a girl's body. Her name was Dawn. *Dawn, Dawn, Dawn what? What was the damned surname?!*

Moore.

Dawn Moore.

I had invited her around under false pretences. I'd met her in a club and given her my number. I invited her out for a meal and said I would pick her up from her home, as I didn't want her having my address. I drove out to her place, collected her and then said I had to go back to mine to collect my wallet. She offered to pay for the meal, as I had paid for the drinks at the club, but I declined.

At mine, I said I wasn't going to be long but that she was more than welcome to step in whilst I looked for my wallet - a little story that I made up suggesting that I wasn't exactly sure where I had placed it. She came in and waited in the living room. It was there that I gutted her with a knife; a slit up her stomach, spilling out the contents. She didn't stay standing for long. She hit the floor the same time as the knife did - dropped from my own hand as I no longer needed it.

Kneeling on the floor next to her, I pushed both hands inside her and started pulling out the internal organs; looking for the liver and kidneys so that I could cook them up to see if they tasted the same as an animal's. I didn't have a fucking clue as to where to find the various organs - a fact made evident when I pierced the stomach bag with an over-zealous reach of my hands. A heavy stink in the air as a yellow bile pooled out onto the floor. I gave up fisting through the bloody mess when that yellow shit spilled out. I just guessed it was never meant to be and so I walked through to the kitchen and prepared myself a sandwich, after a quick rinse under the tap of my hands.

So anyway - back then... *That* hadn't put me off my dinner but today... I glanced back to the *Nutella* spread across the toast.

Shit.

That's rank.

Funny what triggers disgust. I think - today - I'll skip food. I wasn't that hungry anyway... Yep. Not hungry. Just thirsty. I walked over to the sink and poured myself a glass of cold water. I smiled to myself when my brain wasn't able to think of anything disgusting enough to put me off from drinking water.

Liquid diet today.

*

There was a small puddle of sick next to the bed, slowly soaking into the carpet. Had I left it a while longer before coming up, there would have been no trace of it other than the stench hanging in the air; a foul mixture of stomach bile and shit. A smell that - for some reason - reminds me of raw mince. Looking at the vomit, I sighed. I guess she wasn't able to keep it all down after all. Still, I won't discipline her. It doesn't seem fair. Bit like when a puppy does something bad; you don't tell them off unless you catch them in the act. If you do, they just get confused and scared. Both when you're dealing with a puppy and with a woman such as Michelle - especially with what I am asking of her... Discipline would be a backwards step.

'Did you want some water?' I asked her.

I was playing both roles in the *Good Cop, Bad Cop* scenario. Last time I came in here, I was an asshole and - this time - I'm the nice guy. Can only imagine the taste in her mouth; the heavy bitterness of faeces mixed with the sour flavourings of the vomit - retched up from the depths of the gut.

She didn't answer me.

'It's not a trick question. Did you want a glass of water?'

'Water or urine?' she asked - refusing to look me in the eyes.

'Water.'

She didn't answer again.

'You agree to make this film with me and this can all stop,' I reminded her.

'I'm not helping you.'

I sat down on the edge of the bed, despite not being invited to do so. I sat there in silence for a moment unsure of how best to proceed. I didn't understand what her problem was. This was a way out for her *and* she gets to be the star. Why would she not want to take it? What - does she want to end up like one of the other film stars? An extra - killed off and easily forgotten?

I decided to be direct, 'Why won't you help?' I asked a second question without giving her a chance to answer the first, 'What have you honestly got to lose?'

'You want me to love you. You want me to convince you to stop killing people, stop making these movies - and be with me instead?'

'In a nut-shell.'

'I don't want people thinking I love a psychopath.'

I didn't say anything. What the hell could I say to that?

I sighed, 'I'll get you a glass of water.'

I didn't wait to hear whether she wanted it or not. Instead, I turned and walked from the room - pulling the door shut behind me before I found myself saying something stupid that both of us would regret.

*

The water overflowed the rim of the glass and soaked my hand. I snapped back to reality and pulled the glass away from the tap water's steady flow twisting the faucet off with my other hand. I hadn't been concentrating on what I was doing. Instead I had been going through the two options I seem to have laid out in front of me. The first option being to try and convince the girl that helping me is the right thing to do and the second option... Well... *Kill her* and go to the trouble of finding a replacement to be my co-star.

I sighed heavily. I've been gearing up for this for such a long time and now - because I feel like a fraud - I don't know what is going on and what I am going to do. I feel as though I am going around in fruitless circles. Hell - there is even a part of me that...

I glanced towards the knife resting in its wooden block by the side of the sink. So easy to just run the blade down my wrists or across my throat. Moments of pain but then *nothing*. No more trying to make my mark, no more trying to be remembered. I could just fade into nothing and join the rest of the forgotten artists.

I shook the thought from my mind. I am better than that. I am stronger. I am also more patient than this. I have spent so long making these movies, getting ready to make my mark... I can wait a little longer. I promised Michelle a torturous time ahead of her until she agreed. I can't give up and off her after the first attempt at breaking her.

I can do this and she *will* do this.

I left the kitchen with the glass of water in hand. First she gets a drink - staying hydrated is important - and then she gets to see my nasty side again. Good cop, bad cop. Sort of.

'Waterworld'

1. INT. BATHROOM - LATE EVENING

The white ceramic bathtub is in the shot. It is full to the brim with water. Nothing else is in the shot although a lot can be heard; footsteps coming from beyond the room and muffled voices - male and female: One belongs to ADAM, as per usual, and the second belongs to SOPHIE HALL. Like the people before her, she is known as VICTIM. Out of shot, the bathroom door crashes open and someone stumbles into the room, still out of shot.

ADAM

Watch the fucking camera, you stupid cunt!

VICTIM

(scared)

I'm sorry.

ADAM

Shut up.

VICTIM

What do you want from me?

                          ADAM

     Absolutely nothing. Just thought you might need the toilet. Or…

                          (a beat)

A nice bath? No easy way of saying this but you're starting to smell a bit, you know? It's a little

                         off-putting.

Off shot there is commotion; a struggle of sorts. SOPHIE suddenly falls into the shot and slips into the bathtub, face first. She is naked. ADAM pounces and holds her there - her head under the water. She struggles to surface again. ADAM is too strong for her. A few splashes of water hit the camera lens hampering our view. A couple of uncomfortable minutes pass by and - then everything goes still. ADAM turns away from the bathtub and sits on the floor with his back leaning against it. He is out of breath.

                          ADAM

                Cleanliness is next to Godliness.

He stands up and walks from the shot. A rag comes into view and dries the lens off. We can see unobstructed once more. SOPHIE is in the bath-tub. She is face down. ADAM enters the shot once more and turns her over so that she is facing up. Her eyes are wide open. We close in on them.

                                                        FADE TO BLACK

Chapter Nine

A Potential Deal

Michelle was turning her head from side to side trying to avoid the stream but she couldn't. All she did was ensure I managed to get both sides of her once-pretty face. By the time I am done, she looks like a drowned rat. Stinks like one too but that's my fault. There I was lecturing her on the importance of staying hydrated and it turns out I haven't been doing it myself. My piss stinks - as she knows only too well now.

I put my cock back in my pants and took a step back.

'Still thirsty?' I asked - a wry smile on my face.

'Fuck you!' She spat some dark yellow urine from her mouth.

I laughed, 'If you need to brush your teeth… I have the perfect paste that you can use.'

She spat again, not at me - just clearing the taste from her mouth. Her eyes were fixed on me; a definite look of hatred.

'I told you I'm going to carry this on until you agree to help me.'

'Why me?' she hissed.

I was getting frustrated by the she was talking to me. The tone of voice was rude and uncalled for, 'Please stop talking to me like that. It's really starting to get to me.'

'I don't care.'

I bit my tongue. If I answered, I knew it wouldn't be kind. If she knows she can get to me, she'll only carry on. I took a couple of seconds to calm my temper, 'Why you?' I confirmed the question she had asked.

'Yes.'

'Because you're here. It's nothing personal. It really could have been anyone.'

'Then let me go and find someone else.'

I laughed, 'I'm not letting you go.'

'I won't help.'

I shrugged, 'Then we're going to carry on dancing this little dance until one of us dies from old age.' I laughed, 'That's a long way away if we live until old age takes us. I mean - both in our thirties… Could be at least forty years together if you think the average age is around seventy to eighty.'

'I don't care. It means you'll never get your film made…' She smiled at me, 'And people will be looking for me.'

My turn to smile, 'I have killed around twenty people. Only last week did I have a lady back here by the name of Carmen Brooks. She had family too, so she said. You know what I did to her?' No response as per. 'She's dead now. I took her into the garage and I put her head in the vice. I tightened it until her skull cracked. She wasn't dead. I removed her knickers and - with her trapped in place - I fucked her until I ejaculated deep inside of her tight, tight cunt.'

'I don't want to know this…'

'Garden shears.' I continued, 'That's what I used. I mean - after I ran ice along her nipples to make them erect. She had lovely nipples.' I laughed, 'If you want to see them - I can show you. I kept them. The only part of her that I did keep. You see, once they were erect I put one of the shears' blades either side of the nipple. And then… Slowly… I squeezed the garden shears' handles together. She screamed, boy did she scream…'

'Why are you telling me this?'

'That was last week. Other than a few reports on the news, waffling about how concerned her family is and appealing for witnesses… They have no idea where she is. And, they have no clue that - when I had finished cutting her nipples off - I continued turning the handle of the vice. You know, as she screamed, her nose erupted in blood and her eyeballs literally popped from her head. It was pretty messy but incredibly satisfying.'

'Fuck you.'

'So people might be looking for you but they won't find you. And I won't stop tormenting you.'

'Fuck you,' she repeated.

'You have incredibly limited vocabulary, don't you?' I went back to my reminiscing, 'Can you imagine the coldness of the blades against your skin? Can you imagine the pain when they first begin to pinch together? What about the sting that accompanies the final snip.' I shrugged, 'Maybe you won't have to imagine it. I still have the shears down in the garage. I can easily go and get them.'

'Fuck you.'

I put my hand between her legs and she squirmed despite not being able to get away from my touch. 'Fuck me? How about fuck *you*?' I smiled at her, 'Maybe that's what you need to start falling in love with me. Maybe you need to feel how loving I can be?' She didn't say anything. I think she was starting to figure it out now; she told me to eat shit, I made her eat shit literally. She said fuck you… I threatened to fuck her. 'You're going to help me. I don't know why you're putting yourself through this. The way my story ends - with the two of us in love… It works. It also means there is no more torture. There is no more pain…'

'Instead I have people think I'm part of your sick games. I have people think I ended up with a fucking psychopath as a boyfriend. People will think of us as the new Fred and Rose West…'

'There! You said it yourself! People will *think* of us… Don't you want to be remembered?'

'Not like that!'

I paused a moment. Needed a little time to think things through. Was that the issue? Was she worried about being remembered as someone who was crazy enough to fall in love with a serial killer? She didn't want people thinking she was capable of loving someone like me? If that was the only reason she wasn't going along with the plan then there was a simple explanation which I thought she would have already realised.

'Behind the scenes footage,' I told her.

'What are you talking about?'

'There's footage which will show you were forced into this. You're merely an actress in my film.' I pointed towards the CCTV camera. 'And don't forget the other camera I set up when you had… your dinner. It's all filmed, it's all documented. I will be putting the behind-the-scenes stuff on the disk, along with the main film. People love that kind of stuff…' I paused a moment and explained it in simpler terms for her, 'So - yes - on the film you will make it look like you love me but, there will be footage showing how you came to agree to be in the film. It's simple.'

Michelle didn't say anything for a moment. I could see by her face that she was thinking things through slowly.

'Just think,' I continued, 'it could lead to a career in Hollywood. People will see your acting skills and believe you actually did love me. They'll be lining up with movie roles for you and television deals and…'

'Fuck you.'

I sighed.

Stupid woman.

'You have one hour before I come back up here and give you a manicure.'

'What?!'

'I noticed your nails are getting long. I'm going to leave you here for a minute, to think things through, and then I'm going to come up here and give you a much needed manicure.' I smiled at her, 'Have a think.'

I turned the bedroom light out and stepped from the room, closing the door behind me and plunging her into blackness. There are no distractions when you're in complete darkness; nothing to get in the way of thoughts - both clear and cloudy.

Chapter Ten

The Editing Room

I feel nothing when I take the life of another person. To me they are merely actors for my films. I do not think of their families at home. I do not think of their loved ones waiting to see if they're going to walk back through the door or whether their bodies are going to be found. I'm surprised that I even remember their names. Sitting here, watching the saved movie files on my computer, trying to decide which ones need to go in my film - I feel nothing but surprise. Surprised by the fact that I can pull their names from the back of my mind where I thought they'd long since been forgotten.

Katie Rock is on screen. I don't remember where I found here, I don't remember bringing her back to my house and yet - her name... Soon as I saw her face on the screen, up popped her name at the forefront of my mind. As I watched the clip, I remembered how much I liked this one. It was simple yet effective.

Katie was on the garage floor. Both of her legs were twisted around from where I'd broken them by slamming the sledgehammer against them repeatedly until *that* satisfying crack echoed around the room. She was crawling towards the garage door. It was closed so I'm not sure where she thought she was going exactly. It certainly wouldn't have been easy for her to reach up and open the garage door with the automated button on the wall. Not with those legs.

I fast forward the video until... *Ah ha.*

I am sitting in the car. A nice angle caught from a CCTV camera hanging from the corner of the room. I am smiling. The engine is on and I am audibly revving the car. Katie is screaming for someone to help her even though - before the cameras rolled - I had told her that no one could hear us. Either she lived in hope or she didn't believe me.

The car jolted forward a fraction.

Here we go. This is my favourite bit now.

The camera angle changed as the car continued to inch forward - slowly. The camera angle was taken from the floor near to the garage door - positioned in such a way that she was crawling towards us. The pain is evident in her face; her mouth is stretched open, her eyes are screwed up tight with tears glistening on her cheeks. And yet - the expression is about to get much worse for her as the car wheels mount her legs. Over the next couple of minutes the car works its way up her body; up the legs... The bones are cracking with each movement.

I stopped the film.

That's a given for being included in the main feature. I dragged the file from that folder back across to the desktop. I'll create a separate sub-folder soon; *Feature*. It's not the first file I have dragged over. Katie Rock joins Becki Lee's film - a two minute segment whereby I plugged her into the mains and fried her until she first started to smoke and then caught fire. By the time we were done, she was black. Or rather, she was chargrilled. A spoiled piece of meat left too long on the grill.

Clicking back into the previously created folder, containing the rest of the files, I clicked on the next one down. A box opened up on screen and - a second later - the movie started to automatically play.

Jennifer Kampfschulte.

I stopped the film immediately. I don't need to watch it to know it gets included in the main feature. I dragged the file across to where the other two were waiting. She had been a foreign lady living over here. An accent to her voice that I couldn't place.

In the film, I had forced her mouth open and pulled her tongue out. Using scissors, with serrated edges, I had slowly cut her tongue out of her mouth. I filmed this one months ago. In fact, it was one of the earlier films I put together and yet - right up until last week - I sometimes replicate the feeling. How? I roll three pieces of ham up so they're in a long roll and then I use the very same scissors to cut slithers off. It feels the same. It sounds strange but you can feel it in your fingers. You can hear the sound of the meat ripping. It's… *satisfying.*

Okay. Three films chosen. A good start.

I'm thinking that the film will start with me talking to the camera. Maybe something about wanting to bring horror back to the mainstream and my original plan of wanting to do that with the little films that I was making. Then, after a montage of the pre-made horror films, the camera comes back to me and I say something like, 'I never expected to find love.'

Immediately the audience knows there is horror coming their way but that there is more to the story than just that. There is a love interest. Straight away, their curiosity is piqued and they have a reason to carry on watching. I'll introduce the girl that is winning me over and play through those scenes. Then, when I am on camera alone, you can see how conflicted I am… I want to carry on making my films but… I'm starting to feel something for this supposed-victim. I'll be in bed, tossing and turning, and there'll be more horror montages spliced with footage of me struggling with what to do.

The more I think about it, the more I realise I could be onto something special here.

I just need the stupid bitch to agree but… I'm starting to get a good feeling about her. I told her that I can make it clear in the behind-the-scenes footage that she isn't really my girlfriend, just so long as she behaves herself and makes the real film look convincing. I need her to look like she actually loves me or it won't work.

Well, it has been an hour.

I pushed myself away from the computer desk and swivelled around. A glance up towards the ceiling and a sigh. On the other side of the ceiling panel was her bed and where she was waiting.

Let's go and see whether she has changed her mind…

'Nails'

1. INT. SPARE BEDROOM - LATER

The camera is set up so that we have a close-up of one of MICHELLE'S hands. It is palm down, on the bed, held in place by one of ADAM'S hands. MICHELLE'S nails are painted a reddish colour and are badly chipped. Around her wrist - just about visible underneath ADAM'S hand - is a binding that we already know is keeping her on the bed, stopping her from running away from the house of horrors and back to her waiting life.

                ADAM

So what's the answer? Are you going to help me? I've made it clear that people will know you were merely acting the part.

                MICHELLE

I don't want to do it. Just kill me. Get it over with. We both know you're not going to let me go.

                ADAM

I've told you, I'm not going to kill you.

                (a beat)

I'm going to keep you as my own little play-thing.

MICHELLE

(crying)

Please just kill me.

ADAM

Anyway, I noticed your nails… They're getting long…

MICHELLE

Please…

ADAM

When nails get too long, they're unattractive - don't you think?

MICHELLE

… Don't do this.

ADAM

I'm not doing it. You're doing it.

(a beat)

You can make this all stop. Just tell me you're going to do the film.

ADAM'S other hand enters the shot clutching a pair of pliers. He attaches the head of the pliers onto the nail of MICHELLE'S index finger. MICHELLE is visibly trying to move her hand but to no avail; it isn't going anywhere all the time ADAM is holding her there.

                    MICHELLE

            Don't do this. Please.

                    ADAM

        These pliers have seen a lot of action.

                                    CUT TO: -

2. INT. GARAGE - EARLY MORNING

A WOMAN is tied to a chair. There is a gag in her mouth. The camera sees her from a head-on view. The scene is shot in black and white signifying a flash back. ADAM steps into the shot with the same set of pliers as seen in scene one. He walks up to the WOMAN, DEBBIE DALE, and removes the gag from her mouth. She goes to say something but is stopped when ADAM grabs her face with his hand. He squeezes her cheeks together, revealing her teeth, and sets the pliers upon one front tooth. He grips hard whilst she struggles beneath him, her eyes wide with fear. With the tooth gripped hard, he twists violently and she screams out in pain as blood pours from the gum-line. ADAM twists back the other way. There's a loud crack as he pulled the tooth - root and all - from the gum's bloody socket. He drops the tooth on the floor and moves the pliers to the next one available.

CUT TO: -

3. INT. SPARE BEDROOM (scene 1 'Nailed' continued)

We are back in colour. MICHELLE'S pinned hand and ADAM'S hand (with the pliers) are still in the shot, with the pliers still firmly attached to the nail. ADAM pulls the pliers away from the hand, ripping the nail from the finger. MICHELLE screams.

ADAM

We have nine more to go yet.

(a beat)

Remember - you can stop this at any moment just by agreeing…

MICHELLE is wailing. ADAM attaches the pliers to the next finger. The first finger is bleeding profusely. He grips hard and - for a second time - tugs the nail from the finger; a tiny piece of skin left hanging from the edge of the nail. MICHELLE screams louder, having not stopped screaming from the ripping out of the first nail. He opens the pliers up, dropping the broken nail onto the bed, and selects the third.

MICHELLE

Wait! Wait! Please!

ADAM

You'll do it?

MICHELLE doesn't answer fast enough. The third nail is pulled from the finger and she screams out again. Before she finishes screaming, ADAM selects the fourth nail.

MICHELLE

I'll do it! Please! Stop! I'll do it!

ADAM smiles.

FADE TO BLACK

Chapter Eleven

And Introducing

I had turned the camera off. It wasn't needed to film anymore but I didn't put it away. It's tucked away in the corner of the room, ready to film our first proper scene together. She is still in the belief that I am using the behind-the-scenes footage to prove she was an unwilling partner in all of this but - little does she know - that won't be the case. I'll keep the footage but it will be encrypted for my benefit only. The general public will never get to see it. They will simply believe she loved me and I fell for her. And here is how...

'I'm going to come into the room with - I don't know - a blowtorch, or something. Okay? You're going to be in the bed, as you are now. I'll stand at the foot of the bed and I'll be menacing... But... You're not going to be scared. You're going to recognise me. You've seen the reports on the news about a serial killer snatching people from the streets and torturing them before disposing of their broken bodies... It's a simple set up; you're basically a fan of what I do - much like how I feel for Arthur... You don't want to be killed by me... You want to *help* me.' I stopped talking and calmed myself down. I was getting too damned excited at the prospect of taking the film to the next level. Meanwhile she was looking at me with a blank expression on her face. Her eyes red from the crying. 'Did you hear me?'

She nodded.

'So what do you think?' Getting excited with the idea again, I carried on, 'I mean there will be more to it than that. I'm not going to just untie you and start a romance with you - no - that would be silly. Instead, it's going to awaken a part of me I never knew existed, you know? It's going to make me feel something new inside of me. I'll realise what it means to be loved and how it makes me feel inside, gradually overtaking the need to kill and hurt people but there will be some great scenes of conflict going on.'

'When will you let me go?' Michelle asked.

I didn't answer her question. I barely even registered it. I was more interested in getting the first of the scenes shot so that I could start editing it together to see how it's going to look; get an early impression. It doesn't matter that she looks as though she has been crying. Reason being, she would look scared had she just woken, tied up in a stranger's bed. If anything - the red eyes add to the scene.

I reached for the camera in the corner of the room and set it up to the side of the room. I have the CCTV camera capturing every moment anyway but we will also film this scene from various angles and then I'll edit it together as best as I can. I did a film course once which stated the more camera angles there are, the more expensive looking the production is. No idea if it is true but - better safe than sorry.

I aimed the camera so that it would capture the bed in the foreground of the shot and the door - where I'll be - in the background. A quick check through the viewfinder and it's looking good. Admittedly I don't get her face in the shot, she'll be looking away from me, but that's why I will film from the other angle too - a close-up of her face.

'Do you understand what you need to say?' I asked her.

'We have to do it now?'

'No time like the present. Sooner we get it done, the sooner we can wrap up.' Going from the expression on her face, I'm not sure if she registered the words at all, 'Do you understand that?'

She nodded.

'You want to get it done sooner rather than later?'

She hesitated a moment before nodding again. I smiled. The correct response from her.

'You remember what you need to say? You recognise me from the news?'

Again, she nodded.

'Well then,' I smiled, 'let's start!'

I double-checked the camera's shot once more before turning it on. It didn't matter that it would capture me leaving the room. I can edit that bit out. Satisfied it was recording, I walked out of the bedroom and crossed the hallway into the other bedroom. Lined up against the walls in the second room, a choice of props including the blowtorch I'd earlier considered. I grabbed it from the shelf and paused - a thought popped into my mind.

Tara Tannenbaum.

I had used a blowtorch before in another film. A film starring Tara as the victim. She had been unconscious when I used it, having passed out from the pain already dealt, but it was still a used idea and I don't want the film to be repetitive even if it was good to use.

I smiled as I remembered what it had done to Tara's eyeball. Damned thing bubbled up and everything, as the skin around the eye socket blistered. In fact, so impressed was I - I boiled the second eyeball too. All captured on camera.

I surveyed the shelves before me and the various props on display. They weren't items any more, they were people. A battered old chainsaw became Colleen Cassidy, the woman I split from vagina upwards - turning her into a woman of two halves. The little packet of darts next to it became Sandra Dawson, the woman strapped to the wall with a dartboard painted on her face. An afternoon spent using her as target practice until I grew tired and used… The samurai sword next to the darts also became Sandra. A quick slice across her neck separated head from body and gave me something else to play with. Her head became my new football.

Hurry up and pick something already. The fucking camera is rolling. Besides - it's not something that's even going to get used. Not yet anyway.

I grabbed a dildo from the shelf. A black nine inch beast. Into the tip of which I had previously inserted razor blades. A few practise swings and I walked back through to Michelle's bedroom where the camera caught my dramatic entrance.

'Indecent Proposal'

1. INT. SPARE BEDROOM - LATER

We know how it is set up in the spare bedroom. MICHELLE is in the bed. The camera - a wide shot - captures both her laying there and ADAM as he enters via the bedroom door, a weaponised-dildo in his hand.

                    ADAM

          Oh good. You're awake.

                  MICHELLE

       Who are you? What do you want?

                  ADAM

            (ignoring her)

Was starting to think you weren't going to come to.

                MICHELLE

             Where am I?

              (a beat)

         Please, let me go!

ADAM

Yeah - sorry - that's not going to happen.

MICHELLE

Please - I have a family.

ADAM

(shrugs)

As do most of my house guests.

The camera angle changes to a close-up of MICHELLE'S panic-stricken face. A sudden look of realisation hits her out of the blue.

MICHELLE

Wait - I know you…

ADAM

What?

MICHELLE

You're on the news at the moment. You're the serial killer they're talking about.

The camera angle changes back to the previous shot, capturing them both.

ADAM

(smiles)

They're talking about me?

MICHELLE

On all the channels. They're saying you're the most prolific serial killer the United Kingdom has ever seen.

ADAM

You seem to know a lot…

MICHELLE

I've been following the story. I…

(pause)

I've always been fascinated by serial killers.

ADAM

(laughs)

And now you're going to die by the hand of one of them.

ADAM walks to the bed. He sits next to MICHELLE and runs the dildo up her legs. He is smiling - not a happy grin but a sadistic one.

ADAM

The first time women have sex, they feel a sting…

(holds up the dildo)

I won't lie… You're going to feel a sting.

Razor blades in the tip of the dildo catch the light and give off a shine that is uncharacteristic for the product in question. ADAM sets the dildo to one side for a moment and rips MICHELLE'S leggings down as far as possible, exposing her shaven pussy. He looks at it and gives a nod of approval before picking the dildo up once more. Another glisten from the razors.

MICHELLE

Wait. Please… I can help you!

ADAM

Help me?

(laughs)

Why do I need help? You just said it yourself - I'm the United Kingdom's most prolific serial killer. Why would I need your help?

MICHELLE

Imagine the numbers you could reach if you had help.

(a beat)

Please. I've been watching the reports. I've studied people like you in the past. Books, documentaries, films… Whatever I can find. I devour it all. Please - people like me - we're not supposed to be the victims. We're supposed to be the accomplices. Please don't do this. I can be of use… Just think about it… Please…

CUT TO BLACK.

Chapter Twelve

Critics and Warnings

I watched back the first scene we shot together for my film. It wasn't bad but the last part needed to be edited out; the section after her spiel about telling me to think about it. After that, the scene kind of lost direction. I tried carrying it on but she didn't really know what to say. I wasn't angry. Considering there was no script, she did pretty well even if she was a little wooden. That's something that can be fixed in time though. I can coach her on how to act. After all, I learned all about it at school. She needs to put herself into the role and believe she is the character she is portraying. Like I said, something that can come in time. First, we need to finish the first scene. I need to give her pointers on what else to say.

Thinking of where we can go from where it left off - clearly I need to ask her what she can do for me. She then needs to tell me that she'll be good at getting people to the house so I don't have to go out as much. Less chance of me being spotted somewhere if there is more than one person snatching the victims. I'll tell her I don't trust her and can't just let her go because she'll go straight to the police. I'm not that stupid after all.

I guess, from there, she would tell me she can gain my trust by killing someone. She'll take a life if it means I spare her own life. I have no doubt she will kick off when I mention this to her but she doesn't need to kill someone - it's just a line that she'll say to try and convince me to spare her.

It's all pretty simple really or rather, it's simple for someone like me. It's unfair to expect her to be able to ad-lib all of that. This is all new to her and I have to keep that in mind if this is to work and I'm to keep my patience. So long as she listens to what I have to say and then repeats it for the camera, as though they're her own words, we're golden.

I laughed.

Debra Bergevin.

I gave Debra words once. I filmed myself being interviewed by a lady. The camera was in close-up of my face and her face. She was asking questions - in a rather masculine voice - and I was answering in a similar voice. In my head the scene worked really well but - the reality - it wasn't that great.

A second camera shot revealed the truth of the setting. I was sitting there with my hand up inside the bloody, hollowed-out neck-stump of Debra. My hand up inside her mouth. My fingers pressed against the roof of her mouth and my thumb pushing down against her tongue. If I moved my thumb down - away from my fingers and the top her mouth - she opened her mouth. If I closed my thumb back up against my fingers - she closed her mouth. Worked that bitch like a puppet.

Like I said, it worked well on paper but in reality… It was fun, despite her saliva sticking to my hand like mozzarella cheese, but… Just didn't work.

Back to the scene we filmed earlier today though; credit where it is due - what we have so far - it's pretty good. It's certainly a decent start to the process. With a smile on my face, I closed the editing program down. As I did so, an email pinged through; a notification appearing in the top right hand corner of my screen letting me know that it was there. Amazon.

I opened my emails and - sure enough - there was a new message waiting for me from Amazon; a little head's up that Matt Shaw has released a new book. In no rush to do anything else, I followed the link to what was being offered and - immediately - I had that sinking feeling in my heart again. Shaw had written a book called "Don't Read" and the synopsis read as though it is based on the serial killer Michelle had told me about.

Despite being pissed off, I still found myself clicking to purchase it for later reading. I don't even know why I am pissed about it, my plans have changed now so it doesn't matter that some hack writer is bringing the serial killer back into the limelight. This... What I am doing here now... This can't be considered the same thing as he had allegedly been doing. Although - I have to confess - with limited information available due to the fact that most of the evidence had been destroyed by the fire, it will be interesting to see how Shaw filled in the missing blanks.

I wonder...

When my film comes out...

Will Matt Shaw write a book about me? I'd rather it were Bray. Or a combined effort perhaps? Maybe I should get in touch with them and see whether they'd be up for it. They're both reachable through social media although - need to concentrate on getting the film finished first. No sense picturing the end-game when I don't even have a finalised product to offer anyone.

I closed the emails up and re-loaded the editing program again. I'm not tired and there is nothing else to do so I might as well carry on working on the film. I still need to figure out how to start it off and I think - thanks to being reminded of Matt Shaw's books - I have the perfect way.

I need to start it off with a warning. A message saying that it's sick. To accompany the message, I have the perfect clip, - something to really drive the point home and give the pussies out there the opportunity to turn off before I corrupt them. Give them no excuse to leave a bad review because the contents are 'sick' and I - the creator - am clearly a deranged individual.

I minimised the editing software and opened the folder of clips.

Where are you, you son of a bitch?

Ah ha. Middle of the collection. A file labeled S.B.A.G.

Sarah Bullen and Angela Gillmore.

'SICK'

1. INT. MAIN BEDROOM - LATE EVENING

SARAH BULLEN (VICTIM 1) is standing next to the bed. ANGELA GILLMORE (VICTIM 2) is tied to the bed in a spread-eagled position. Both girls are naked and visibly scared - not helped by the fact ADAM is standing behind SARAH with a knife blade pressed against her neck. The scene is captured by the camera on a tripod, at the foot of the bed. Classical music plays softly in the background of the shot from a source unseen.

>   ADAM
>
>   (menacing)
>
>   Do it.

>   SARAH
>
>   (To ANGELA)
>
>   I'm sorry.

>   ADAM
>
>   (insistent)
>
>   Shut up and do it!

Shaking, SARAH puts her fingers in her mouth. She hesitates and then gags before violently spewing up over ANGELA'S naked body. ADAM pulls the knife away slightly, careful not to get a splash back of sick on his hand. He is laughing. The vomit - mostly liquid with a few chunks of the mushed-up and half-eaten chicken dinner she'd eaten earlier - lands on ANGELA'S belly. ANGELA is screaming.

                      ADAM

                    (still laughing)

              In her face. Get it in her face!

                      SARAH

                      I can't.

ADAM puts the knife up against her throat once more. He presses it so hard that the knife cuts the skin slightly.

                      SARAH

                    Okay! Okay!

                 (to ANGELA again)

                     I'm sorry.

> ANGELA
>
> (crying)
>
> It's okay.

ANGELA knows there is little choice in SARAH'S actions. She isn't accountable. He is. SARAH puts her fingers in her mouth for a second time and pushes them down the back of her throat until she - again - gags and vomits over ANGELA'S face. Most of the sick is kept from ANGELA'S mouth by the fact she keeps it closed.

> ADAM
>
> No! No! No!
>
> (a beat)
>
> Do it again and this time...
>
> (to ANGELA)
>
> Keep your fucking mouth open!

ADAM presses the knife against SARAH'S skin once more as she puts her fingers to the back of her throat for the third time. A second later and ADAM cheers as SARAH vomits directly into ANGELA'S mouth who - in turn - is also sick; a fountain of stomach bile with slithers of what looks like carrot spraying up into the air before splashing back down on herself. Both women are screaming as ADAM continues to cheer at the chain reaction caused. He then gags but holds in his own vomit.

ADAM

Yes! That's what I am talking about!

SARAH

Why are you doing this?!

ADAM

Kiss her.

SARAH

What?

ADAM

(pressing the knife against her again)

I said "kiss her".

SARAH, weeping, bends down so that she is face to face with ANGELA. A look on both of the girls' faces - an unspoken apology for what they are being made to do. That mixed with fear. SARAH closes her eyes and puckers up her lips before quickly kissing ANGELA on the mouth. ADAM shakes his head again

ADAM

No, no, no, NO!

(a beat)

That won't do. That won't do at all.

He steps away from the girls and grabs the camera from the tripod. He moves it so that the shot is now hand-held, in close-up of ANGELA'S sick-drenched face. We can see the detail in the vomit; bits of froth, food debris, spittle and stomach lining. We can just imagine the smell, similar to a full bin rammed with leftover foods and general month old waste.

ADAM

(sinister)

With tongues.

(to ANGELA)

And you kiss her back.

SARAH

Please don't do this to us.

The knife comes up into the shot and points at SARAH. SARAH flinches although no further movement is made.

ADAM

This isn't a question of choice. Kiss.

SARAH leans down close to ANGELA'S face once more. The camera moves closer. SARAH retches in ANGELA'S face who - in turn - gags back. We can hear ADAM laughing. Both women slowly part their mouths as SARAH moves closer still.

ADAM

I want to see passion. The *audience* wants to see passion.

Just as SARAH is about to make her move, ANGELA vomits directly in her face. Another chain reaction as SARAH sicks up again - also in ANGELA'S face. The screen pauses; both girls have grimaces on their faces, both girls are dripping in vomit.

SCREEN FADES TO BLACK

Chapter Thirteen

Moving on

Another day gone and more progress made on the film. I'm feeling good and Michelle is playing her part as well as can be expected.

The warning is at the start of the film and it looks great. It's a simple black screen with white writing explaining that what the viewers are about to see, is sick. It goes from there straight to the video of Angela and Sarah vomiting over each other and kissing the bitter juices back out of their mouths only to then violently be ill over one another again. I find it difficult to watch, what with having a weak stomach for that kind of thing, but - at the same time - kind of humorous too. It's certainly a good telling of the kind of imagery that's to be coming throughout the rest of the film.

From there the film cuts to a close-up of me. I look good on camera. My eyes - despite them appearing black in most photos - have a real depth to them. It is like you can - for once - see into my soul and it's not as black as pictures would have you believe. I do believe I carry a kind of charm too, especially when I smile - which is something I do often in the introduction as I explain who I am and what I am doing.

I give my name. I say that I want to be known as the most prolific serial killer across the globe, not just the United Kingdom, and I give a montage of videos showing people I have already killed. Not the complete scene. It wouldn't work if I did the whole scene. It's just glimpses as to how the people died, just as the scene with Sarah and Angela wasn't the complete scene. I mean, the whole scene shows how they die but there's little point in keeping that in. It's not necessary for that part of the film. I want to show the film as sick, I show a scene of sick. Put their deaths there - quick cuts across their throats - and it would confuse the initial message of the scene. But I digress. The montage… The montage shows how people died but it doesn't show the conversations I had with them to start off with. For example - when I threw the cup of acid in one victim's face, the audience of my film do not get to see the conversation we had beforehand where I teased him with the promise of release. It's not needed. I merely tell the camera - in a face to face - that I kill people, then I show them me *killing* people, and then the camera cuts back to me and I say the line, 'Whilst doing all of this - whilst pursuing my dream - I never expected to find love'. It is at this point we cut to the first scene between Michelle and myself.

I think - so far - it's pretty powerful stuff and that was exactly what I had told Michelle.

'And last night I filmed myself in bed - tossing and turning, thinking about our conversations. Again, I'm going to splice some of the murder footage in with that along with footage of you saying you have feelings for me.'

The footage where Michelle said she thought she had feelings for me was the last thing we filmed together last night. I told her that I didn't believe her, that I felt she was just trying to save her own skin. She said she would kill someone to prove she isn't trying to get away from me. Prove her love - and loyalty - by taking another life. It sounds weird talking about this scene now but it will make sense when it is put into the film properly. It's rare that movies are filmed in chronological order.

'So what happens now?' she asked. 'When can I go home?'

'We still need to film the sex scene. We need to film me laying here with you. We need the audience to see my feelings for you grow. And then - of course - we need to film the ending.'

'How will it end?' she asked.

I smiled at her, 'I don't want to spoil it for you.'

The camera was set up in the corner of the room, waiting to be turned on to capture the scenes planned for today. She doesn't know this yet but I'm going to film my segment now. I'll be sitting on the end of the bed with my back to her. I'll be in the foreground of the shot and she will be in the background. I'll be upset. She'll just be listening to what I have to say; a tragic story of how I've never been loved by anyone. Not properly. And that - what I am feeling inside now - I do not understand and how I worry that she is trying to trick me. All she needs to do is tell me that everything will be okay and - in time - she'll prove she loves me. Again, she'll offer to take someone's life at this point of the film. A belief that if she was trying to trick me and she was a normal person looking for a way out - they wouldn't willingly take the life of an innocent person.

At the end of the scene I'm going to run from the room, still confused and feeling vulnerable at being seen like this.

Now, most of the talking is down to me and I've been going through what to say over and over again in my head so - fingers crossed - it should be relatively simple. *Should be.* So long as we get it done in a timely fashion, we might even be able to film the sex scene later before she gets anymore… un-fresh.

I told her the plans for the day, 'I want to film a short piece with me sitting on the end of the bed, my back to you, saying that I am scared because I've never felt these feelings before. By the time we're done - it should be quite a vulnerable scene for me.' I explained the importance of getting the scene right, 'This will be the first time the audience will see this side of me. Up until this point, I'm just a murderer but with this… It gives me another dimension.'

'It would if it were real,' Michelle said in a matter of fact tone.

I shrugged, 'To them - it will be real.'

I've never had a girlfriend that I didn't pay by the hour for. Well… There was that one girl but… I don't like to think of her like that anymore. I didn't love my parents. I don't even respect them, especially my father. When I kill women, I don't think of anyone in particular but the men I've killed... I've always pictured them as my father. In fact - thinking back to the bigger picture - I don't think I've ever loved anyone.

My pet cat, even she isn't loved.

She is merely tolerated after I adopted her from the Rescue Centre. It wasn't planned. I simply woke up one day and headed to the centre and pointed to the first cat I saw. It was my attempt at fitting in with society. Normal people have pets. Now I have a pet too. I never loved her though. The only reason I didn't wring her scrawny neck was because people hate cruelty to animals - even horror lovers.

I changed the subject, 'So what do you think? You think we can get this scene filmed quickly? Be another one in the can and another step closer to being finished.'

She didn't answer me. Usually when I suggested we filmed something she agreed more or less straight away - especially when I hinted to us being another step closer to being finished - but not this time. It was clear from her face that she had something on her mind.

'What's wrong?' I asked.

'You mentioned a sex scene?' She looked nervous.

I nodded, 'You love me, I think I am falling for you. It makes sense that there'd be a sex scene.'

'I don't...'

I knew what was about to come out of her mouth. She was about to say she didn't want to do it but we both knew that wasn't a choice, 'Be careful of the next words out of your mouth,' I warned her.

She didn't say anything.

Michelle needs to get on the same page as me. When that scene is filmed, it needs to look as though we do love each other. If she looks scared, it will ruin the whole illusion. And considering the romance between us is the heart of the film, if the audience doesn't believe it, the picture will not be taken seriously. I just hope that - when the time comes - she manages to find a way to get through it. If not... I guess we'll have to film some more behind-the-scenes-footage.

'How's about we concentrate on the scene at hand first?' I suggested for fear of having the whole day wiped out due to her nerves at the upcoming sex scene. 'Just me sitting on the edge of the bed explaining that all of this is new to me... All you have to do is reassure me you're not trying to pull the wool over my eyes, you're being genuine and that - if need be - you will happily kill someone to prove your devotion. To me - I am your John Lennon. I am your God...' Much to my relief she was nodding. 'I'll get the shot set up properly and then we will have a quick run through before actually recording, okay?' She nodded for a second time.

Whatever else happens with this day - at least this scene will be in the bag. Also, with some trick photography, there may be a way around having to film the sex scene with her. I mean, if she does a good enough job with everything else, I could film me on top of her - pretending to have sex... Making the motions and sounds. She'll have to play along and moan with pleasure too but, I might not have to show the penetration. It all depends on how Lauriette Hutzler is keeping.

Lauriette is a girl I brought home and murdered after having intercourse with her. Another cheap whore plucked from the streets. These girls make the best dates because they rarely have anyone reliable at home waiting for them. You can pluck them from the streets and no one cares.

She actually surprised me. I say 'she' but it wasn't her as a person that took me by surprise. It was actually her pussy. Her cunt was so tight and so satisfying to fuck that I actually sawed the top of her body away - from the belly button upwards - and then cut away from the top of her thighs on each leg leaving me with just the mid-section of her body to keep and cherish forever. My own easy to clean sex-toy.

Hopefully keeping her in the fridge, ready to warm up when feeling the mood for it, means her vagina is still fresh enough to look good on camera. I could splice together the footage of me pretending to hump Michelle with footage of me sticking it in what used to be Lauriette's gash. With clever editing there is a good chance the audience will never know but that's only if I have to. If Michelle says she is up for it and is willing to put in an Oscar winning performance then there is no reason not to bareback her.

Time will tell I guess but no need to rush ahead in my mind. Bring it down a level or two and get this scene filmed. After all, this scene is just as important for it shows the audience that - actually - I do have it in me to be human.

As I started to set the camera up, Michelle and I ran through the scene.

'Something Inside'

1. INT. SPARE BEDROOM - LATER

ADAM is sitting on the edge of the bed facing the camera. MICHELLE is behind him, slightly out of focus yet it is obvious she is looking at him, listening to what he has to say.

ADAM

I'm not sure what is happening in my head. I know that I shouldn't listen to you. I know that I should just kill you and - yet - I can't. I don't know, maybe I've had enough of the killing? Maybe I yearn for the company of another? Maybe I… These feelings inside me, I've not experienced them before. They're new to me and I don't even know if they're real… And if they are… I can't be sure that what you're saying is the truth. It could be a trick just as I have tricked so many before.

MICHELLE

It is the truth. I've followed everything you do, whenever it was reported. I know it's wrong but I love how your mind works. You live in a world I wish I was part of. I know you have no reason to believe me, or even trust me but… Like I've said before - give me a chance and I'll prove myself to you.

(a beat)

The next person you bring back here, let me kill them. I can't very well be released and run off to the police if I have taken a life…

(pause)

MICHELLE (continued)

I mean it, just give me the chance to prove myself. That's all I ask. And then, when I do, let me help you with what you want to achieve. We could be the perfect partnership. We could be a new Bonnie and Clyde or a better looking Fred and Rose...

ADAM

(starts to laugh)

A better looking Fred and Rose? You want us to be married?!

MICHELLE

Well - no need to rush these things but I like you.

(a beat)

I really like you.

ADAM turns to her.

ADAM

And I think I like you.

                    MICHELLE

                    Kiss me.

                    ADAM

                    What?

                    MICHELLE

                    Please.

ADAM moves up the bed. The camera angle changes to that of CCTV footage captured by the camera hanging from the corner of the room. ADAM is on top of MICHELLE. This is not a passionate scene. It's awkward and clumsy - mainly because ADAM is out of his comfort zone. He cannot remember the last time he had a willing partner. Even so - he kisses her. A poor, sloppy attempt before a second - better one. He quickly pulls away and rips MICHELLE'S leggings down to her knees. Due to the restraints, he can't pull them off completely. Her cunt is exposed and he admires it for a second before - like an intrigued school boy - touching it tentatively. MICHELLE both flinches and sighs.

                    MICHELLE

                    Do it.

                    (a beat)

                    I want to feel you inside me.

ADAM gets up from the bed and undoes his trousers, freeing his erection. He stands there a moment with MICHELLE'S eyes fixed on his member.

MICHELLE

Fuck me.

The camera angle changes to a close up of a cunt. A penis enters the shot and pushes against the vagina before sliding in - working against the friction. When it slides back out (not all the way) it is glistening with wetness. It pushes back in once more - a strange scene given that there are no sounds other than the wet sound of repeated penetration.

FADE TO BLACK.

Chapter Fourteen

A Needed Break

I pushed what used to be a normal toothbrush up the vagina used for the sex scene and scrubbed up inside - gently so as not to cause any real damage but with enough pressure to clear away any semen that hadn't trickled back out. I hadn't meant to ejaculate in there but it had felt so good I couldn't help myself. I pulled the brush out and ran it under the sink before putting it back in the cup where I kept my own toothbrush. They're different colours so no chance of getting the two confused not that I would be too put off if I did.

Satisfied the insides were more or less semen free, I gave it a rinse using the shower-head that hung over the bathtub. Some of the warm water works its way up the various channels and trickles straight out of the midriff area where I had cut the rest of the body away. The water went in a crystal clear colour and came out tainted brown and red. Probably safe to assume it's no longer considered to be safe drinking water - unless of course you're African. They drink anything they can get their hands on.

I put the cut-away section of Lauriette down in the tub to allow it to dry. It has been a while since I had pulled that out for a fuck and I have no idea why - still feels as good as it had the day I first penetrated it, when the rest of Lauriette was still attached to it. Not entirely sure where this film is going now although I have some ideas but - if it requires another sex scene - I'm definitely going for the ass. Can only imagine the tightness on offer there given the way the vagina clenches my erection.

I felt a surprising twitch from between my legs. Usually, when I've cum, I don't need to do so for days afterwards. I'm not a highly sexual person. Yet the thought of how tight her pussy is and how tight her arse could be... Well... Another twitch suggests I could go again if time wasn't against me. Maybe a little treat to myself later on, depending on how well the editing goes.

After hanging the shower-head back up on the wall , I left the bathroom and hurried back to Michelle. With some key scenes in the bag, I want to spend a few hours working on what happens next in the film and - of course - double-checking where I am at so far. Need to make sure I have everything planned out and that everything done so far is of a decent standard because once I get to the end - if it ends how I think it will - it will be very hard to go back and do re-shoots. Before I do any of that though, I need to see if she is hungry yet and willing to eat something.

Poor girl hasn't eaten since I fed her excrement. She must be starving.

I stopped in my tracks and about turned back towards the bathroom.

Need to brush my own teeth. Forgot she'd eaten shit. I kissed that. I thought it tasted funky. I just presumed it was morning breath. Clean forgot that it was most likely actual shit. Should have inspected her mouth first. Guessing the worst of it - what made it obvious that it was there - has come away due to repeated licks of her own tongue in a desperate bid to clean herself up. Jesus. I fucking kissed that.

Back in the bathroom I reached for my toothbrush.

*

I walked into the spare room. Michelle was still laying there, tied to the bed with her leggings half-way down her legs and her pussy exposed. The second thing that I noticed were that her wrists were starting to look sore. No doubt she has been struggling against them again. She must realise now that they're not going anywhere and yet she is still trying. I'm not sure whether to be impressed with her determination or frustrated that she doesn't accept she isn't going anywhere until I say otherwise.

'I just came to see if you wanted something to eat,' I offered. 'No tricks, I promise. We did well today - got a lot filmed.'

'I'm not hungry.'

'You need to eat.'

'Please can you pull my leggings up? I'm cold.'

I nodded, 'Okay.'

I walked over to where she lay and reached down to the top of the scrunched up leggings. Taking a hold of them I froze a moment with my eyes fixed on her slit. Another twitch as I imagined myself sliding inside her. She lifted herself up off the bed slightly giving me a better view of her opening, even though I knew that wasn't her intention. She was merely trying to make it easier for me to redress her.

I shook the perverse thoughts from my mind and pulled the leggings up. We're so close to filming the last scene that I don't want to ruin it all by fucking her. I will - however - fuck the living shit out of her when we're done. A post-wrap treat to both myself and her.

Back to the matter at hand, I asked her again, 'Can I get you something to eat? I'm going to make myself something.'

She shook her head again, 'I'm not hungry.'

'Not even a little bit?' I smiled, 'I have some microwave roasts in the freezer. Birdseye no less.' A taste for which I had grown accustomed to having read about Peter Jenkins' fascination with them in Shaw's *Happy Ever After*. The way the character harped on about them, I had to give them a try to see what the fuss was and - actually - I've been hooked ever since. A couple of minutes in the microwave and, before you know it, you're tucking into a tasty dinner that's both satisfying and filling. He's right about the supermarket own brands though; they're shit.

'I just want to go home.'

'I understand that,' I was growing frustrated, 'but as I said before - we have a film to make.' So as not to upset her, or make her feel like there was no point in carrying on, I did promise her, 'We're nearly done though. Promise.'

'And then you'll let me go?'

I smiled at her. 'Are you sure I can't get you something to eat? Like I said - I'm getting myself something so it won't be any bother and, promise, no tricks.'

'Answer the question,' she suddenly demanded.

'Have dinner with me and I'll answer all the questions you have. You need to eat something or you're going to make yourself ill.' It was a comment that I found quietly amusing considering - before - I had made her eat something which *did* make her ill. 'Does that sound fair?'

'I don't have a choice, do I?'

I smiled again. Now she's starting to get it. 'Not really.' I headed back towards the bedroom door and said over my shoulder, 'I'll get dinner.' I stopped a moment and slowly turned back to Michelle, 'You can eat it up here or I can take you downstairs to eat it but - I have to warn you - if you try anything…' I stopped. Were the words really necessary? A hint is enough, surely. 'We're in a good place at the moment and we are nearly finished. Let's not ruin this working relationship, yeah?'

She nodded and I smiled. I don't think she'd be so stupid but I felt it had to be said.

'I'll come and get you when everything is ready.'

'And I need to go to the bathroom again too,' she said quietly.

I nodded. It's not the first time she has needed to go to the bathroom. Previous visits, I kept her ankles and wrists shackled but this time - maybe that won't be necessary? Maybe.

'I won't be long,' I told her.

*

The bathroom door opened. Michelle looks as though she has not just gone to the toilet but tried her best - with the limited supplies in there - to give herself a quick wash too. Certainly her mouth is cleaner now. She stepped out towards me with her wrists pushed together - ready for me to cuff her again.

'I don't think that's necessary now,' I told her. I gestured towards the stairs with a sweep of my arm, 'After you - dinner's already set up down there.' I let her lead the way; an illusion of freedom despite the fact I have a knife tucked into the back of my trousers. She tries anything, film or no film - she's going to get stuck. She walked down the stairs. 'Turn right and then it's the first door on the left,' I informed her. She followed my instructions and entered the living-room-come-dining-area. True to my word, two roast meals were waiting for us over on the dining table. 'Take a seat,' I told her in a tone which couldn't have been considered too pushy. I waited until she took her seat and then I sat opposite her, pulling myself - and my chair - closer to the table.

'Looks nice,' she said.

I'm not sure if she is being genuine or simply speaking for the sake of it. I'll give her the benefit of the doubt, 'Birdseye. Had to give them a go after reading about them in a book... This character was infatuated with them and I needed to see what the fuss was about. Been eating them ever since.' I smiled at her and continued, trying to get her to relax further, 'Never know - you might get a taste for them too.'

I picked my knife and fork up and started eating the meal whilst it was still warm. A few seconds later, she started eating her meal. I watched her as she slowly chewed - almost as though she didn't trust that I hadn't tampered with the food. Silly really considering I let her choose which seat to take. There was no way of me knowing which she would go for.

'Nice?' I asked her.

'It's good,' she replied. Again, is she being polite? Possibly but it has to taste better than shit, right? She took another mouthful and chewed - a little less slowly this time. It's nice to see her eat. First proper thing that has gone in her mouth for a while now. She swallowed hard and went to say something but stopped herself. She shovelled more food in her mouth hoping I hadn't noticed. I had.

'What is it?' I asked.

She swallowed again, 'I just wondered when you think we'll be done.'

'I have an ending in mind,' I told her. 'It's simple and wraps things up nicely. If you want - we can film it after dinner.'

She pushed again, 'What is it?'

'Uh uh uh, spoilers.' I ate a little more of my own dinner. She was looking at me, hoping for an answer. 'Tell me about yourself,' I told her - after I swallowed my current mouthful. 'Tell me about yourself,' I said again, 'I *want* to know who my co-star is...' I paused. She didn't look as though she were about to offer up any information so I gave her an incentive, 'You answer my question and I'll answer a question from you.'

There was a brief silence. I took the opportunity to have a mouthful of potato.

'What do you want to know?' she asked.

'Anything!' I swallowed. 'Tell me about yourself. For example - what are your hobbies?'

She shrugged, 'I don't know what you want me to say...' She thought for a minute, 'I like reading...'

'That's a start. Good. What else?'

'I like walking - generally exploring the outdoors. I enjoy swimming and arts and crafts... I love watching CSI programmes and horror films and gory stuff in general...' She shrugged and suddenly got herself wound up, 'I don't know what you want me to say!'

'That's good. See - immediately I feel like I know you a little better.' I tried to keep the conversation flowing, 'What about horror films and gory stuff? You never said you enjoyed them! So, this film - the one we're making - sound like something you'd watch?'

She ignored my second question and turned the tables back on me, 'I answered your question. You have to answer mine. That was your rules to this *game*.'

Of course. You're right. I'm sorry. So - yeah - okay... I'll answer your question. Shoot.'

'How much more until we're done?'

A flash of anger rushed through me and I slammed my hand down on the table - clenched fist - causing Michelle to jump. 'Of everything you want to ask me, that's the fucking question? Come on, try again. You can get to know me. No one else usually has this chance and no one else *will* have this chance. Come on... You must have a better question than that!' I felt myself ranting so made a conscious effort to shut my mouth.

Michelle squirmed in her seat. I could see it on her face that she was desperately searching for something else to ask; something else that wouldn't get the same negative reaction from me. Come on, girl, make it a good question.

'How did you go from being a filmmaker to a murderer?' she asked with a stutter of nervousness in her voice. I stopped chewing the food I had just forked into my mouth. I had asked her about her hobbies and she had come straight out with *that* for a question. It was clear from the look on her face that she immediately regretted asking it. Too late now. Can't take it back. I'll play nice though. Fair is fair. I'll answer her question.

'Her name was Dawn Cano,' I started.

'Vision'

1. INT. FLAT LIVING ROOM - LATER

The camera sits on a tripod capturing most of the room. There is a settee in the background of the shot where DAWN CANO sits. ADAM is in the foreground of the shot reading through the instruction manual of the camera. DAWN looks bored.

                        DAWN

            Are you going to be playing with that thing all night?

                        ADAM

                 I'm just making sure it works.

                        DAWN

                I can't believe you bought it.

                        ADAM

       Can't very well move forward with a career without one, can I?

                        DAWN

                      Yes but…

ADAM

(turns to her)

But what?

DAWN

It's a lot of money.

ADAM

Which will be made back when I sell my first film.

DAWN

You haven't even written a screenplay though. What exactly are you going to film until then?

(a beat)

And then - how are you going to make your film? You can't very well make it with no money, can you? Not forgetting your lack of cast and locations and…

(frustrated)

Just forget I said anything.

ADAM

(disappointed in her)

Really? You sound like my parents.

DAWN

(changing the subject)

Come on - I invited you over to spend time with you not watch you read a booklet…

ADAM

I thought you were happy I wanted to do this? I thought you were the one person who got me?

DAWN

I am. I'm just worried that…

(looks to camera)

It's a lot of money.

ADAM

Which I already told you I will be making back!

DAWN

Come on - put the booklet down…

DAWN stands up and snatches the pamphlet from ADAM'S hand.

ADAM

Give that back.

DAWN

Only if you promise to put it away.

(a beat)

You can go through it when you're at your own house! You don't have to…

DAWN screams out with playful laughter as ADAM pounces on her, wrestling her for the book. She tries to hide it behind her back but he reaches round and tries to take it back. Whilst she thinks it is all playful and fun - the look on ADAM'S face suggests he doesn't find it funny and, more to the point, he is getting angrier by the minute. With little warning, like a spoiled child, he yanks DAWN off the settee. She lands hard on the floor.

DAWN

(in pain)

Ow! What the fuck!

ADAM

I told you to give me the fucking thing.

(a beat)

That was your fault.

                    DAWN

                  Fuck you.

             (under her breath)

              Fucking psycho…

                    ADAM

    (angrily hitting her head back against the floor)

          Don't call me a fucking psycho!

By the time he stops, DAWN is not moving.

                    ADAM

                    Dawn?

                  (nothing)

              Stop fucking about.

                  (nothing)

              Open your eyes.

                  (nothing)

                    Dawn!

Blood trickles from both of her nostrils. He checks for a pulse. There is nothing. He looks at the camera - shock on his face and horror that he has accidentally killed her.

CUT TO: -

2. INT. FLAT LIVING ROOM - LATER

ADAM is sitting in front of the shot. We are in extreme close-up of his face so nothing else is visible. Despite having just killed his girlfriend, there are no tears in his eyes. He looks cold. He looks distant.

ADAM

I know you won't believe me when I say it was an accident. I know I am going to jail and nothing I can say will change that. What's more - I know it will be for the rest of my life. Certainly for the best part of my life. I'll go to prison and no one will remember me. Which is why… If I am going to prison…

(a beat)

I want to be remembered.

(a beat)

And the only way to do that is by making a film that will go down in history and… I see how.

(a beat)

I see how to make this work.

CUT TO: -

3. INT. FLAT LIVING ROOM - LATER

We are in close-up of DAWN'S face. Her eyes are staring directly at us, unblinking.

                    ADAM (out of shot)

    Dawn would never have understood or seen the way out that I have seen.

                    (a beat)

            Because she lacked the vision…

ADAM'S hands come into the shot. We realise we are in the POV of ADAM and move closer to DAWN'S face as ADAM'S hands reach out and touch either side of her face with the thumbs over her eyes.

                    ADAM (out of shot)

              She has aways lacked vision.

His thumbs pressed into her eyes. We hear a squelch noise as her eyeballs are pushed back into the skull. The screen freezes…

Chapter Fifteen

That's a wrap

I paused the playback of the DVD. I had explained what happened to Dawn before putting Michelle back in the spare bedroom and had felt the inclination to watch Dawn's video once more. I've lost count of the number of times I have seen it. When I first watched it, I was proud. Now, though... Now... I turned the film off. I don't want to watch it anymore and - out of respect to Dawn - I won't put it in the film. Just the DVD extras with other un-used footage; a little bonus to the people good enough to get a copy of the film.

The footage of Dawn continues with me pressing her eyes back into her brain. By the time I remove my thumbs, you can barely recognise what was left behind as anything resembling eyeballs. They look like jellied-mush. Bits of gore hanging on my thumbs which were then cleaned using the front of my trousers.

Like I said in the film - and also admitted to Michelle - I had never meant to kill Dawn. It was an accident and - also mentioned in the film - I knew people wouldn't believe me. I would be sent to prison and there was nothing I could do to change that. All I could do was make the film so bad, so grotesque, that people wouldn't be able to forget it, or me. Whenever they shut their eyes, they'll picture what I did in the film. So - yes - I didn't mean to kill Dawn but, everything else that I put her through afterwards was intentional and done for shock value. I pushed her eyeballs into the back of her brain, I cut her tongue out as a warning to those who speak out saying I will never fulfil my dreams, I cut her breasts off and kept them by my computer as stress-relievers - inspired, in part, by the decoration kills of Ed Gein. And then -

later - I fucked her too. All of it was caught on camera for the viewers before I disposed of the body and went home, expecting a knock on the door.

But no one came. There was no knock. There was no one looking for her. No family, nothing. I mean we had only been dating a short while but... She had no relatives? No one to raise the alarm for the police? Or was it that she never spoke of me so no one knew to come with questions? And the body - no one discovered where she was buried?

No one came! Of course I was going to carry on making the scenes. The original plan, to be remembered, was a good one. Especially when all that stuff about Arthur J. Hopkins hit the headlines. I could have been just like him. So... That was the story... The first kill was an accident but it put me on the path that I was on until... Well... Until Michelle swayed me off it.

Michelle.

My mood keeps fluctuating. One minute I think this film is going to be an immense experience for those watching it and then, the next minute, I feel as though I am making a massive mistake and it's all Michelle's fault. Had she not thrown me the curve-ball - about how I was nothing but a cheap copycat - I would never have doubted myself. In fact, I'd be done. More or less.

I should have just killed the bitch. But then, I guess, had I done so... My work would have been remembered for the wrong reasons. I wouldn't have been a success. I would have been a laughing stock. A cheap copycat who'd soon be forgotten.

I sighed heavily.

I'll feel better when I have the final scene is in the bag. Wouldn't even be having these doubts if it weren't for Michelle reminding me of Dawn. Now I'm back to wondering whether Dawn and I would still have been together - living a normal life - had it not been for my temper.

Maybe I'd even have a proper film career? Admittedly I'd most likely be on the bottom rung of the ladder but at least I would be on it!

Jesus what is wrong with me? Get these thoughts out of my head. I can't turn the clock back. I can't bring Dawn back. It's done. I'm done. This is what I am doing now. This is my job. My purpose. I need to get these thoughts out of my brain once and for all and finish this damned film.

I got up and stormed up the stairs, through to the spare bedroom - accidentally startling Michelle as I walked in.

'You scared me!' she said.

I didn't answer her. Not in the mood to talk at the moment. I just want to get the film finished. She doesn't know the ending I have planned. I can't tell her because it will ruin the surprise and I won't get the necessary look of shock on her face which I am hoping to get. No reason I shouldn't get the required reaction.

'Are we filming again?' she asked me. Again, I didn't answer. Besides - I thought it was pretty obvious what was happening, given the fact I was setting the camera up at the foot of the bed having dragged it (on the tripod) from the corner of the room.

A quick check through the view-finder and all was good.

'What's this scene going to be?' she tried again to get me to talk. 'Do I need to say anything particular for you?'

Satisfied with the camera angle, I walked from the room leaving the door open. I need to fetch a prop before we start and - also - the scene requires me to burst into the room, catching her by surprise once more.

I crossed the hallway back to where I keep the props both used and intended for my films. In the corner, on the floor, is the knife I was looking for. I bought it back before I started on this dark path and, even then, I only purchased it because I happened to notice it in a shop I was browsing through. I never intended to go out looking for it and knew I wouldn't have a need for it immediately. I just knew that, if I didn't get it there and then, I wouldn't have been able to find it when I *did* need it. That's how Sod's Law works.

I picked the knife up and gave it a couple of practise thrusts. I had forgotten how damned good it feels in the hand. It has a healthy weight to it, much like a top quality kitchen blade. With a smile on my face, I charged back through to the bedroom - bursting through the door with the desired effect of scaring Michelle. Her eyes immediately fixed on the blade on my hand.

'What are you doing?' she asked.

This is it. The final scene.

'A Special Place in Hell'

2. INT. SPARE BEDROOM - LATER

MICHELLE is tied to the bed as per the other scenes. She has seen the knife in ADAM'S hand. ADAM, himself, stands in the doorway - the knife by his side. He is making zero attempt to keep it hidden. MICHELLE is nervous. ADAM seems sad - almost as though he has given up.

                    ADAM

           We can't be together.

                  MICHELLE

                What?

                    ADAM

            It won't work.

              (a beat)

The things I've done. People will come for me. For us if you're a part of it.

              (a beat)

      We'll be separated from each other.

ADAM takes one stop closer. The knife's blade catches the light drawing even more attention to it.

>   MICHELLE
>
>   (nervous)
>
>   Why have you got a knife?

>   ADAM
>
>   It's the only way.

>   MICHELLE
>
>   What are you doing?

>   ADAM
>
>   You want us to be together?

>   MICHELLE
>
>   (nervously)
>
>   Yes.

>   ADAM
>
>   As do I.

(a beat)

This is the only way.

MICHELLE

I don't understand.

ADAM

We can't be together here but…

(a beat)

In Hell…

(a beat)

We can rule together.

MICHELLE

(alarmed)

What?!

ADAM

(sympathetic smile)

It will only hurt for a minute.

MICHELLE

Please don't do this. I thought…

MICHELLE'S words are cut short when ADAM dashes across the room and runs the knife across her throat - spilling blood. MICHELLE immediately grabs her throat as she starts uncontrollably hacking. There is both panic and shock written over her face.

ADAM

We'll be the King and Queen.

(a beat)

I love you and will see you on the other side.

ADAM steps away from the bed and runs the knife across his own throat. Blood pumps out as he drops the knife and - then - drops to his knees before finally falling out of the shot.

FADE TO CREDITS

The names of the victims run across the screen from bottom to top. And then - Adam's name and the name of Michelle. Adam's name also comes under *director, story, editor* and *cameraman*. When the writing finishes on screen - everything fades to black. A final title appears: Do Not Forget Me.

Chapter Sixteen

A Twist in the Tale

The film stopped. Everything was silent. I could hear my own heartbeat pounding away in my chest. An uncomfortable feeling of nervous anticipation. I wondered if my mobile phone, recording from the desk in front of me, could pick up my heartbeat or whether it too only got the near unbearable silence.

Someone give me a clue.

Did they like my film or not?

Some of my fellow classmates started to laugh.

My tutor didn't say anything. She had her back to me and was still facing the television screen she'd previously set up at the front of the class. Slowly she turned around and looked at me. I could see she was searching her words for what to say.

The rest of the class were chattering amongst themselves. Some of them were saying they enjoyed the film and others were saying that I was sick and in need of psychiatric help. One smart-arse, a so-called friend on the back row, pointed out that I was already under the care of the university psychiatrist and - clearly - it wasn't doing me any good.

'Well the effects were... *good*,' my tutor said.

Her name was Cheryl Hamilton. A stuck-up bitch who believed romance was the only genre worth taking note of. It's because of her that I included the romantic angle between killer and potential victim. I knew she would hate the horror angle. Especially given the fact she'd hated every other piece I had submitted for the film class but I honestly thought - going with this angle - I might stand a chance of getting a pass.

I don't want to just make a sappy, boring romance; the same kind of film most of the other class had submitted. If I had to sit through one more shitty little predictable romance, I'd be forced to kill someone.

'It had some flaws,' she said. 'For instance, how was the film completed if he slit his own throat?'

'Maybe the police compiled it so people could see what happened?'

My tutor laughed, 'I don't think the police would have released the tapes personally. Certainly not showing all the graphic content you have included. Most of which,' she continued, 'felt slightly unnecessary.'

'How is it unnecessary?' I asked. I thought it was a fair point. I was making a horror film; a story about a murderer who was killing people on camera. It needed to be graphic otherwise it wouldn't have worked. It was the whole point of the film. That's why I called it *Extreme Horror*.

'This kind of film would be considered an underground film. There would be a market for it amongst *some* horror fans; the type of crowd who enjoyed the black cover VHS tapes of the eighties such as *Faces of Death*. It wouldn't get a cinematic release though and if it were given to critics - it would be pulled apart.'

The VHS tapes of the eighties have cult status these days. People remember them. If my film could get to that level, I would be happy. At least it would be remembered unlike the rest of the films presented by my classmates. At least *I* would be remembered.

'You need to come away from this kind of story,' my tutor continued. 'Look at Jennifer's film, for example. A good solid film about love and time-travel…'

'Good? It was like a fucking Richard Curtis film,' I snapped. 'In fact - I'm sure he has already done it and, more to the point, it was shit.'

My classmate Jennifer Pelfrey had submitted a film where the young girl couldn't find love with the man she wanted. She kept making moves to try and get noticed but kept mucking it up. Luckily for her, she had a time-travel machine so could keep going back to try and fix things. However, hilarity ensues when she keeps making things worse and the butterfly effect changes things for the worse.

It was shit.

A bell sounded out in the hallway. End of classes. So they think.

Quickly, I got up and hurried over to the door before locking it shut.

'What are you doing?' Mrs. Hamilton asked.

I smiled at her, 'That wasn't the end of my film ' I said. 'I mean - the world will see it and they'll remember it but only because of what I am filming now.'

'What are you talking about? Stop being stupid and unlock the door.'

'Please stop telling me what to do. Or - at the very least - change your tone.' I turned to Michelle who was sitting at the back of the classroom. 'Ready?'

Michelle smiled at me and nodded before reaching down into a bag nestled between her feet. She pulled out a large semi-automatic rifle. Classmates near her scattered to the far side of the room, cowering.

'This is the real horror of the piece. Every day horror that happens across the world. Pupils being gunned down by classmates who have gone and lost the plot. This is horror.'

'Please - whatever you're planning,' Mrs Hamilton started again.

I silenced her by re-aiming the gun at her head.

'My mum and dad said I couldn't be a filmmaker but - look - I am! I've made a film which - admittedly - you hate but then, that's fine, because you're not my target audience. People will see it. It will get leaked because of what happens here. And it's what is going to happen here which is how I will go down in history...'

Michelle coughed.

'Sorry,' I corrected myself, 'it's how *we* will go down in history.' I paused a moment, 'We will live in prison for the rest of our lives knowing we're famous. We're remembered! We're filmmakers having forged our way into the industry...'

'They won't show the film and they won't release footage of what you do here.'

I laughed and nodded towards my desk. My phone was still recording, tilted up against my books to capture most of the scene. Mrs. Hamilton knew immediately what I was doing. I was filming everything. 'See - we're going to kill you all and, then, we're going to upload the video to social networks - all before anyone can stop us. By the time the police get here, our story will already be out.' I nodded back towards the television at the front of the class, 'And remember at the start of the film when I was there making the film to send off to the news channels?' I started to laugh, 'I posted the DVD to them this morning. It doesn't matter if the police hide that copy... Other copies have gone out.' I confirmed, 'It will be shown and - as I said - we will be famous.'

'You're sick,' Mrs. Hamilton said.

'Don't feel too bad,' I told her, 'you'll be remembered too. Victims are always remembered... Oh, and that reminds me... The victims in the film you've just watched? That wasn't effects. I killed them.'

Michelle coughed again.

'Sorry,' I corrected myself, 'we killed them.' I laughed, 'The only fake parts of that film were the scenes between Michelle and I.'

'Go to Hell,' Mrs. Hamilton snapped. She no doubt realises this is the last chance she'll get to have her say. A funny choice of last words, I'll be honest.

'We will go to Hell and - just as we'll be remembered here - we'll be known there too. And it's all thanks to the skills we learned as part of this adult course so, thank you for that. You made us.'

'I did no such…'

Her words were cut short. The gunshot echoed around the room and my classmates screamed as the front row was sprayed with brain matter and blood. Mrs. Hamilton's eyes rolled to the back of the head and a funny noise escaped her mouth - almost like a last word although I couldn't make it out. She dropped to the floor, face down.

A quick glance to my phone. The camera was still recording. Perfect. I turned to Jennifer Pelfrey who was screaming, just as everyone was. I flashed her both a wink and a smile before squeezing the trigger for a second time. The bullet penetrated her eye and exited the back of her head in a second spray of brain matter. She too dropped - as did more classmates when Michelle opened fire.

The gunshots will continue to ring out, like music to our ears, until we run out of ammo. And then, next to the dead bodies, the guns will be laid down and our hands raised in the air. Triumphant smiles on our faces.

Tomorrow we will be on the news.

For the rest of time, we will be remembered.

Sirens were wailing in the distance as the police sped towards us. Not long now before they storm the building to try and take us alive. I smiled. They won't come charging in - not immediately. They'll be worried we might have hostages, or more ammo. They'll take their time to formulate a plan. Why am I thinking this? Simple really.

Christine Feldon.

I've always had a thing for Christine. As she crawls bloodied and weak - towards the door… I probably have time for one final fuck before I get thrown in jail. The amount of times I have masturbated over mentally penetrating her, it seems fitting that I should - at long last - get to live the experience and feel the tightness of her pussy enveloping my penis.

It's true what people say; filmmakers do get the girls.

Michelle watched on, smiling, as I freed my erection from my trousers.

Christine screamed with what little energy she had left.

THE END

Made in the USA
Charleston, SC
24 February 2016